P9-DGW-759

THE CHRISTMAS DOLL

OTHER SCHOLASTIC PRESS BOOKS
BY ELVIRA WOODRUFF

Novels

The Orphan of Ellis Island
A Time Travel Adventure

The Magnificent Mummy Maker

George Washington's Socks

Picture Book

The Memory Coat
(illustrated by Michael Dooling)

The CHRISTMAS DOLL

~ BY ELVIRA WOODRUFF ~

WORCESTER COUNTY LIBRARY
BERLIN BRANCH
BERLIN, MARYLAND

SCHOLASTIC PRESS • NEW YORK

Copyright © 2000 by Elvira Woodruff
All rights reserved. Published by Scholastic Press,
a division of Scholastic Inc., *Publishers since 1920.*
SCHOLASTIC and SCHOLASTIC PRESS and associated logos
are trademarks and/or registered trademarks
of Scholastic Inc.

No part of this publication may be reproduced, or stored in
a retrieval system, or transmitted in any form or by any
means, electronic, mechanical, photocopying, recording, or
otherwise, without written permission of the publisher. For
information regarding permission, write to Scholastic Inc.,
Attention: Permissions Department, 555 Broadway,
New York, NY 10012.

Library of Congress Cataloging-in-Publication Data
Woodruff, Elvira.
The Christmas doll / by Elvira Woodruff.   p.   cm.
Summary: As Christmas approaches, Lucy, a ten-year-old
orphan living on the streets of London, is overjoyed to be
given the job of sewing hearts on the dolls in
Thimblebee's Doll Shop.
ISBN 0-590-31872-1
[1. Dolls—Fiction. 2. Orphans—Fiction.   3. Christmas—
Fiction.   4. London (England)—Fiction.]   I. Title.
PZ7.W8606Ch   2000
[Fic]—dc21   96-45314
                                                              CIP
                                                              AC

10 9 8 7 6 5 4 3 2 1   0/0 01 02 03
Printed in the United States of America   37
First Edition, November 2000

Art by Troy Howell
The text type was set in 12 pt. Weiss.
The title type was handlettered by Troy Howell.
Book design by Kristina Albertson

With special thanks to Diane Garvey Nesin for meticulously
fact checking historic facts in the manuscript.

To Franny Rose Carlton,
whose heart is mightier
than most

—E. W.

Chapter One

ONG AGO IN LONDON TOWN, AT A TIME
when the muffin man's cries began the
day, and the lamplighter ushered in the
night, two young girls lived together in the bleak,
cold shelter of a public workhouse.

There was no mother to guide these unfortunate
two, nor a father to protect them from the want and
wickedness that washed up on the city's wharves.
Alone and penniless, they had only each other to
turn to. For ten-year-old Lucy Wolcott and her six-
year-old sister, Glory, had lost their parents to the
fever that swept the city in the year of 1848. The epi-
demic struck with such a vengeance, London's streets
were left swarming with orphans.

The two little Wolcott sisters were taken from
their family's home to an almshouse, which in turn
sent them to the public workhouse for orphans at
Grimstone Union. There they remained for five
years. The food was scarce and the bread riddled
with worms. They spent their days sitting on hard

benches, knitting stockings and stitching sacks. Nights brought the torment of bedbugs, and when the girls weren't scratching they found themselves shivering under thin, dirty blankets. Hunger and exhaustion were their constant companions, as was the ache in their hearts for the love they had lost and the home they longed for.

One night, little Aggie Crofter, a girl in their dormitory, developed a cough and refused to eat. Word spread that "the fever" was back in the workhouse. The next morning the sisters awoke to find Aggie lying still in her bed as others looked on with cries and whispers. Lucy saw that Aggie's gentle face was now as blue-gray as the sky outside the long dormitory window. Glory tried to go to her, but Lucy was quick to pull her back.

"You mustn't get too close," Lucy warned her sister.

"But why won't Aggie open her eyes?" Glory asked.

"She'll not be opening them ever again," an older girl whispered. "She's bound for St. Martin's yard now, she is."

"What does she mean, Luce?" Glory asked, turning to her sister.

"She's died in her sleep, is wot she means," another girl replied, before Lucy could answer. "They'll be coming to take her to the graveyard at St. Martin's as soon as Matron hears of it."

"Poor Aggie," Glory whispered, tears welling up in her eyes.

Lucy put her arm around her sister. As tiny as Glory was, her heart was bigger than most twice her size. She and Aggie were the same age and had been friends.

"Aggie didn't suffer, Glory," Lucy said gently.

"Might I kiss her good-bye?" Glory pleaded.

But Lucy shook her head no. "You must say your good-byes from your heart," she said, holding her sister back.

Later that day, as the two sat in a long line of girls sewing rag pieces in the cheerless, dank workroom, Lucy cringed to hear a girl across the table from them coughing into her apron. Another girl at the end of the bench had fainted with fever. Lucy looked down at her sister's ragged, thin dress hanging off her bony little shoulders. At six years old, Glory Wolcott's solemn little face was already darkened with worry, as if life's hardships had left their mark.

What if Glory should come down with the fever? Lucy worried. The little one was so thin already, what would happen if she should stop eating? That evening at supper, Lucy dipped a dirty finger into her watery soup (for the inmates at Grimstone were allowed neither forks nor spoons). Lucy picked out the one cabbage leaf floating in her soup and dropped it into Glory's bowl. As the kitchen help stood in the dining hall and ladled the soup, Lucy searched for the familiar face of her friend, Old Poll. If anyone knew of a remedy to ward off the sickness, Poll would.

Old Polly Connors had been working in the kitchen of the workhouse for much of her life. She was known for her powers of healing and her herbal remedies. Old Poll had taken a liking to Lucy and often added an extra ladle of broth into her bowl.

But as Lucy scanned the flushed faces of the women standing behind the large pots of steaming soup, she could not find Polly's stooped figure anywhere.

"If it's Poll you're looking for, you'll not find her here," one of the women told her.

"Why?" Lucy asked, alarmed. "Where is she?"

The woman shook her head sadly. "She died of the fever, last night in her sleep. It's safer out on the streets now than to be locked up in here each night with this sickness going around."

Lucy felt her chest tighten with fear. If Old Poll couldn't ward off the sickness, how could they?

CHAPTER TWO

ATER THAT NIGHT, AS THE GIRLS HURRIED into their nightgowns in the frigid dormitory air, there were whispers up and down the two long lines of beds. Three other girls had died, and now, little Emma Waverly had grown so weak, she, too, had been carried to the sick ward. All anyone talked about was the fever.

"Silence!" Matron Wicks's sharp voice suddenly brought all conversation to a halt.

Lucy flinched at the sound of it, and Glory trembled beside her, for the Matron was a stony-hearted woman who would happily flog any girl for the smallest offense. Everyone took to their beds, and a fearful silence fell over the dormitory. Even the rat that had come out of its hole by the window held its breath as the Matron's footsteps echoed down the aisle. Not until the candles had been snuffed out and the big oak doors slammed shut did a hushed ripple of conversation resume.

"Luce," Glory whispered as the two snuggled together on a dirty mattress under their thin bedcover. "I'm so frightened for Emma."

"You mustn't be," Lucy told her. "She'll be looked after now that she's in the sick ward."

"And I'm worried about Aggie," Glory continued. "It's so very bitter out. What if she's cold, lying all alone in the graveyard? Do you suppose Aggie feels the frost tonight, Luce?"

"No, I shouldn't think so," Lucy whispered back. "For her soul has gone to heaven and no one is ever cold in heaven."

"I wish I were in heaven with Aggie," Glory said, coughing into her hand. "Then I'd be warm, too."

"Don't say that, Glory," Lucy scolded. She reached over and took her sister's chilled feet in her hands and began to rub them.

"I'll tell you the Christmas story," Lucy whispered. "That should warm you up."

There was a hint of a smile on Glory's dirty face at the mention of the Christmas story. For the little one loved hearing the few memories that Lucy had of their parents and the time they were all a family. Each moment that Lucy could recall was like a gem sparkling before them. And the memory that shimmered most was of one Christmas Eve.

Lucy continued to rub Glory's toes as she recalled it for her now.

"'Twas almost Christmas," she began. "Mother was cooking a plum pudding on the fire and the whole room smelled warm and spicy. Candles lit up the room as gold and bright as day!

"Father's nose was red and his cheeks were cold as he came in the door. He had come from the cook shop with our Christmas goose. Father was a gardener, and there was always money for a fine Christmas feast."

"But you need to say how fat the goose was," Glory reminded her.

"Oh, yes. The goose Father brought was the biggest, fattest goose that ever there was!"

"With dressing," Glory added, coughing into her hand. "You forgot to say with dressing."

"Yes, with dressing," Lucy said. Glory knew the story by heart and insisted Lucy retell it each time, exactly the same way.

"And what about me?" Glory interrupted. "Do tell where I was."

"I was just coming 'round to you," continued Lucy. "You were only a baby, and so you were in the cradle by the fire taking your nap. Not so close that the cinders could catch hold of your dress, but close enough to feel warm and cozy, under your coverlet that Mother had made just for you."

Glory pulled a little tattered piece of blanket from under the covers. "And I have a piece of it here," she whispered.

"Yes," Lucy continued. "You'd be warm and snug under your blanket, and Father would sing you a lullaby until you fell sound asleep."

"And Mother?" Glory asked.

"Mother was in her rocking chair embroidering a tiny blue morning glory on to one of your dresses. 'Morning Glory' was what she called you, just like the flowers Father planted in his garden. And on each of your dresses, Mother sewed a beautiful blue blossom, just like the one I sewed on the underside of your apron hem."

Glory reached for her apron that hung on the iron bedpost and turned up the hem to look at the morning glory embroidered there.

"But my flower is gray," she said.

"Yes, 'tis the only color thread we use here," Lucy whispered. "And I was lucky to be able to pinch a strand of that when I did. So you must remember to never let Matron see it, for if she does she'll know that I've pinched the thread and she'll flog us both, certain sure."

"I won't ever show it," Glory promised. "But do tell the part about Mother's kisses."

Lucy gently smoothed back a lock of her sister's tangled hair. "Every night, before you went to sleep, Mother would kiss you good night. She could never let you fall asleep without kisses. And not just one, mind you, but two," Lucy said, kissing Glory on the forehead. "For Mother always gave one kiss for love and another for luck."

"And now tell the part about my doll," Glory pleaded as she snuggled closer.

Lucy smiled. Her stories got better each time she told them. "Mother gave you a doll for your first Christmas. It was a beautiful doll with golden curls just like your own and the sweetest smile. She even had your special name, Morning Glory."

"And if Mother had lived, I'd have my doll, still. 'Tisn't that so, Luce?"

"Oh, yes." Lucy nodded. "For your Morning Glory was left behind when the people from the almshouse came to take us away."

"But she is going to return to us someday," Glory said, her voice filled with sadness.

"Yes," Lucy assured her. "She will return to us someday."

Glory closed her eyes and Lucy did the same.

Suddenly, the damp chill in the air, the poor ragged bedcover, the memory of the Matron's shrill commands, and the dirty mattress they lay on had all but vanished! In their place was the warm glow of a fire, the sound of their father's lullaby, the feel of their mother's soft kisses, and a beautiful doll called Morning Glory.

CHAPTER THREE

UCY AWOKE IN THE MIDDLE OF THE NIGHT to find three tall figures bent over Sarah Hemley's bed. In the glow of their candlelight, Lucy could make out Matron's frowning face. Two men with cloths covering their mouths stood beside her. Lucy watched in horror as they lifted Sarah's limp body from the bed and laid her on a stretcher. Matron quickly covered Sarah's face with a blanket.

"Poor little thing," Lucy heard one of the men say.

"She's with the good Lord now," Matron said stiffly.

Oh, no, not Sarah! Lucy wanted to cry out. For Lucy and Glory had known nine-year-old Sarah Hemley since they had first come to Grimstone. Like them, Sarah was an orphan. She had lived her whole life within these dreary workhouse walls. And now in those same grim shadows she had died!

Lucy felt a cry welling up inside her, but she didn't dare to let it out. For she knew Matron's birch rod was certain to come down on her hands if she did. And besides, she needed to be still for Glory's sake. Lucy was grateful that her sister was still asleep and was spared the frightening sight.

The strong scent of camphor suddenly filled the air as the small body was carried past their bed. Lucy shuddered and wrapped her arms protectively around Glory's slight frame. But her horror grew even greater as she heard Matron call after the men, "And when you're through with that one, come back, for I'm afraid there's another here as well."

Wide-eyed, Lucy watched as the men returned, this time to little Nora Cooperwait's bed.

"Seems like the good Lord is calling 'em all home tonight," one of the men whispered as he lifted Nora's lifeless body onto the stretcher.

"Please, dear Lord," Lucy prayed. "Don't call anyone else. Oh, please let the rest of us stay."

Later as she lay in the dark, the faint scent of camphor still lingered in the air, and Glory snuggled beside her. But panic began to take hold of Lucy as she thought of those who had so recently died. She thought about Aggie and Old Poll, and about Sarah and Nora. What frightened Lucy most was how fast they had perished after only a few days' illness.

And what about the two empty beds Glory and

the others would discover on waking? It terrified her to think of how many more beds would be empty by week's end. With her fears mounting, she began to think more and more of running away.

Lucy had heard stories of the few children who had fled from the workhouse and were caught, only to be returned and punished. The Matron liked to tell of the floggings they received, how their meals were withheld, and how they were thrown in the "keeping room," alone in the dark for days.

"Alone, except for the rat," Matron would always add darkly.

Every girl at Grimstone had heard tales of the keeping-room rat. The rodent was said to be bigger than a cat, with a strong appetite for human flesh. There were stories told of children who had come back from the keeping room with bloody stumps where fingers and toes had once been.

These stories were enough to keep most of the girls from ever dreaming of trying to leave. But Glory was all Lucy had in the world, and no floggings, or hunger, or flesh-eating rat could be worse than losing her little sister. Running away was all she thought about now.

As she closed her eyes, Lucy could hear the familiar night sounds of the wind whistling through the cracks in the dormitory walls and the scritch-scratch of the rats as they scurried under the beds. These had been her only lullaby for the last five years.

But as much as she hated the dismal life at the workhouse, the thought of leaving filled Lucy with fear. She knew that it would take all her courage to push aside those fears of the unknown world outside. And only if she could, was there hope for a better life.

Lying in the dark, Lucy imagined the sound of the rats under her bed turning into the twitter of birds and the whistling of the wind. The sounds then softened to a summer's breeze rustling the leaves of a tree overhead. For as she drifted off to sleep, Lucy often dreamed herself into a garden, her father's garden. It was a place filled with flowers and sunlight. There were no bad smells, just the scent of the earth and the perfume of blossoms. And Lucy always felt safe and happy there.

Whether her father really had been a gardener, Lucy couldn't say for sure. One of the older women at the workhouse said she thought there had been some mention of the girls' father being a gardener, when the sisters first came to Grimstone, though the woman couldn't swear to it. It was the only shred of information Lucy had about her family, and so she clung to it dearly.

As she fell deeper into sleep now, Lucy slipped her hand into her father's large palm and together the two walked down the garden path. "Come, look at the lilies," she heard her father whisper. "Aren't they lovely, Lucy?"

Chapter Four

T BREAKFAST, MATRON CALLED FOR A MO-
ment of silence. She commanded everyone to pray "for the deliverance of Sarah's and Nora's souls."

A collective gasp could be heard in the room, though Matron Wicks's hard face showed no sign of emotion. Her voice revealed no hint of sorrow. Everyone's eyes turned on Matron Wicks's assistant, Mistress Branch, who had just come from the sick ward. Lucy held her breath as she watched Mistress Branch lean over and whisper in Matron's ear.

"It has come to my attention that we should offer a prayer for the soul of another as well," Matron abruptly announced. "For it seems Emma Waverly has joined Nora and Sarah in heaven this day."

Another fearful wave of silence swept through the room. Lucy reached for Glory's hand under the table. Later, as the two made their way in the long line of girls to the workroom, Glory tugged on Lucy's skirts.

"Does everyone die who gets sick?" Glory whispered.

"No, only those who haven't the strength to fight off the fever," Lucy answered.

There was a short pause as Glory thought this over and began to cough. "And are we strong enough to fight off the fever, Luce?" she asked.

"Why, of course," Lucy was quick to assure her. "We're two of the strongest girls in all of . . ."

"In all of Grimstone?" Glory whispered.

"In all of England," Lucy told her, gently running her hand over the little one's great mop of tangled blonde curls.

If only we were the strongest girls, Lucy thought. For as she looked at her sister's frail figure, she couldn't help thinking how helpless Glory looked.

Just like a doll, Lucy thought, looking down at Glory's tiny rosebud mouth and large blue eyes. *A real porcelain doll.* Lucy's own features were much broader, and though she too was thin, her wide features gave her a more solid look. With her head of chestnut hair and freckled nose, Lucy appeared unlike her sister in every aspect, except for the cornflower blue of their eyes.

As the two continued down the long hallway, a girl at the front of the line suddenly fell to the ground in a faint. Matron hurried to the child's side and ordered everyone to stay where they were. Then she sent an older girl to summon the doctor.

Talk of the fever spread quickly down the line.

"We're all going to catch it," someone whispered.

"There's no escape," someone else cried.

"Silence! Be still!" Matron Wicks's voice cracked like a whip, setting them all to trembling. No one dared to say another word.

"You are to return to your dormitory and wait there," Matron instructed. "Keep to your line, with eyes straight ahead. I shall send the doctor down to inspect all of you as soon as he's through here."

It wasn't until they had reached the end of the hallway that someone was brave enough to whisper, "What do you suppose is going to happen now?"

"The doctor shall look us over, and those showing signs of the sickness will be taken away," an older girl said.

"Taken where?" Lucy turned around to ask.

"To the sick ward," the girl said with a shrug.

"As good as sending you to your grave," someone else added. "No one ever returns from the sick ward alive anymore."

Everyone grew quiet as they passed the closed doors of the sick ward. And though no one said her name, Lucy knew they were all thinking of poor little

Emma Waverly. When Glory began to cough, Lucy looked back anxiously.

"You mustn't do that when the Doctor examines you," Lucy whispered in Glory's ear. "You mustn't cough, and if he asks you how you're feeling you must tell him you feel fine. Do you understand, Glory? 'Tis very important."

"Yes, I . . ." Glory tried to answer, but was overcome again by her coughing and could not speak.

"That's all right," Lucy said, patting her back. "Try to get it all out now, so that when he comes you'll be still. You must be still, Glory, you must."

Lucy pulled her close in a hug. The two had never been apart. And Lucy knew that if they were to be separated now it could be forever. She closed her eyes and prayed, as she listened to the rattle in her sister's chest grow louder.

CHAPTER FIVE

 NCE THEY WERE BACK IN THE DORMITORY, Glory lay down to rest while Lucy stood at the long window beside their bed and worried. She could not see outside the window, however, as last spring the medical officer had inspected the building and ordered all the windows to be whitewashed. He told Matron that sunlight carried disease. Matron said she thought that was rubbish, but it wasn't her place to argue with the medical inspector. And so no rays of light were allowed to enter, throwing the dormitory into perpetual gloom.

With her thumbnail, Lucy scratched at the glass now, until she had made a small circle. Through this she saw a row of rooftops, and in the distance she could see the city. Her heart leapt at the sight of it. It was like looking at another world, for she had almost no memory of ever living outside of the workhouse.

If only there was a way we could get to the city, Lucy thought now. *Maybe we'd be safe, away from the sickness and away from the evil-smelling men who come for you in the middle of the night. If only we really were the strongest girls in England, we could escape this place and never look back.*

"Luce," Glory suddenly called from the bed. "I'm afraid, Luce. I'm afraid they're going to send me away."

"Don't you worry, Glory," Lucy said, sitting down on the bed beside her. "You'll make your cough worse."

"I don't want to be away from you, Luce," Glory whimpered. "I won't be able to sleep without you near."

"You won't have to. I promise," Lucy said, trying hard not to cry herself. She wiped Glory's wet cheek with the edge of her frayed skirt. "I'll tell you a Morning Glory story. That will cheer us up."

Glory's head of dirty curls bobbed up and down between her sniffles.

"Once there was a little girl called Glory, who had a beautiful doll," Lucy began, lying down on the bed beside her sister. "This doll was named Morning Glory, and she was a wonderful doll, unlike any in all the world . . ."

Of course, Lucy had no memories of their ever owning anything as fancy as a doll. In truth, she could only remember seeing a real doll but once in her life. It was during Christmas week, two years past, as she and Glory marched with ten other orphaned girls through St. James's Park. Each year the very wealthy Lady Raisley sent for twelve orphans to be brought to her house to receive a Christmas gift. There the grand lady handed out a new set of shoelaces to each orphan. It was the only gift they would receive from anyone all year.

Lucy and Glory were beside themselves with excitement for they were rarely let out of doors and never into the park. It was there, on the park's gravel path, that Lucy spied two fashionably-dressed girls pushing a little wicker pram. As Lucy got closer, she saw the most beautiful sight she had ever seen. It was a porcelain doll with golden hair and rosy red cheeks. She was dressed in a gown of garnet satin and lace.

Lucy had been so taken by the doll, it took a sharp whack to the back of her neck from Matron's birch rod to remind her to get back in line. She had had only a moment to look at the doll. But from that one moment, Lucy was able to fashion a series of stories that would entertain her sister for many an hour thereafter.

"Glory loved her doll so dearly," Lucy continued, "that it was a dreadful day when they were separated."

"And Morning Glory was so sad that she wanted

no other little girl to find her. Isn't that so, Luce?" Glory whispered.

"Yes, 'tis true," Lucy agreed. "And so Morning Glory kept herself hidden away so that no one should find her."

"No one but me," Glory added.

"No one but you," Lucy nodded.

"When?" Glory murmured. "When will I find Morning Glory?" She closed her eyes as she snuggled closer.

"I can't say when, for I don't rightly know," Lucy said, keeping an eye on the big oak doors. "But someday, when you least expect it, why, there she'll be. As soon as you see her, you'll know, for your heart will recognize her. And she'll be yours to keep forever and ever."

Lucy often wondered if perhaps she was doing wrong by making such a promise. For she knew that it would be nearly impossible for Glory to ever own anything as grand as a doll. Still, it was the hope of it all that seemed to cheer Glory so. And Lucy could not resist the chance to make her sister happy, even if it was only with made-up stories.

"Tell about Morning Glory's smile," Glory pleaded now, as she lay with her eyes closed.

"Oh, it was a lovely smile," Lucy continued. "But it

curved up ever so slightly at the side. And this caused Morning Glory to have a look that seemed almost wise. It was this special smile that Glory liked most about her doll. And she grew to love Morning Glory more than anything in the world. . . ."

"'Cepting her sister," Glory suddenly interrupted.

Lucy smiled. "'Cepting her sister," she added. "Now, Glory never went anywhere without her doll. Until one day . . ."

"Hush, all of you." An excited voice suddenly broke the spell of the story. "Matron is on her way! And I see the doctor with her."

Glory's eyes opened wide as Lucy turned to see Matron Wicks and the doctor enter the dormitory.

"'Tis all we'll have time for now. I'll finish telling you the rest at bedtime, tonight," Lucy whispered, trying hard to keep the nervousness out of her voice. She helped Glory to stand beside the bed. "Now you must remember not to cough and to . . ."

"I'm afraid, Luce." Glory began to whimper again as she clung to Lucy's arm. "Oh, don't let them take me away!" She began to cough.

"Oh, Glory," Lucy pleaded, "you must try very hard not to cough, and I'll tell you more about Morning Glory. Close your eyes now and listen."

The little one did as she was told, but still clung tightly to her sister's arm.

Lucy felt her mouth go dry as she watched the doctor follow Matron Wicks from one bed to the next. "'Twas the most perfect day," she managed to whisper in Glory's ear. "Glory and her doll were walking in the park. The sun was out, but it wasn't carrying any diseases that day. It felt warm and good on Glory's face. She could smell the grass and flowers and see the sky above her head. And when she looked down at her doll she . . ."

"She smiled," Glory finished, her eyes still closed.

Lucy looked at her sister and was relieved to see that she had calmed down.

"Aye, she smiled," Lucy whispered.

"Wolcotts, step forward," Matron Wicks's sharp voice suddenly crackled in Lucy's ear.

With her heart pounding in her chest, Lucy took hold of Glory's hand and stepped forward.

Please, Lord, Lucy prayed silently. *Please don't let them take her. . . .*

But it was a prayer that was left unfinished, for no sooner had the doctor laid his white bony fingers on Glory's shoulder than she began to cough.

CHAPTER SIX

HE DOCTOR FROWNED AS HE LOOKED IN Glory's frightened eyes. "Send her to the sick ward at once," he said.

"And the other?" Matron Wicks asked, with a nod to Lucy.

"She seems fit for now. No need to fill up the ward."

Lucy started to object, but she was immediately silenced by the sound of Matron's birch rod hitting the iron bedpost.

"Enough!" Matron Wicks snapped, glaring at Lucy. "There will be no discussion. See that the child's nightdress is sent with her."

Lucy felt Glory's fingernails digging into her arm as she watched Matron Wicks and the doctor move on to the next bed.

"I shan't be coming back," Glory said in a faraway voice. "Emma didn't, and I shan't, either. . . ."

"Don't say that, Glory!" Lucy cried, grabbing hold of her sister's thin shoulders. "You *will* come back. I won't let you end up like Emma and the others." Lucy pressed her lips to Glory's forehead. "I'll find a way for us to be together," she whispered. "I promise I will."

Glory was silent as her red-rimmed eyes met Lucy's.

"I'll *never* give up and you must promise that you won't either," Lucy said, hugging her close.

Glory nodded her head, as a large tear rolled down her cheek.

"Better hurry," a voice suddenly called to them. Lucy turned to see an older girl waiting to take Glory away.

"I'm just fetching her nightdress," Lucy said, reaching for the tattered nightgown that hung on the hook by their bed.

"Remember what I told you," Lucy whispered as she placed it in her sister's trembling hands.

Glory was about to reach out for Lucy's arms, when the older girl grabbed her hand and snatched her away.

"We'll both be sent to the keeping room if we don't hurry," the girl scolded. "I've three others to fetch, so come away with you now."

"Please keep your promise," Lucy whispered, as she watched Glory being led through the oak doors.

Later that night, long after the other girls in the dormitory had fallen asleep, Lucy tiptoed down the long aisle between the two rows of beds. Somehow she was going to get Glory and escape from the workhouse.

Reaching into her apron pocket she felt for the pair of scissors she had forgotten to return to the workroom that afternoon. She would bring them along. Perhaps they would come in handy. Beneath the scissors, in the same pocket, was a dirty little scrap of blanket. She would bring that, too.

Lucy's heart pounded as she reached the big oak doors. Taking a deep breath, she quietly pushed one of the doors open. It creaked loudly, and her heart pounded harder. Quickly, she slipped out through the opening and hurried down the darkened hall toward the sick ward.

Once there, she could smell the sharp scent of lye in the air. Lucy squinted as she tried to find her bearings.

"Glory?" Lucy whispered in the dark as she reached the first bed. But then she saw a head of black hair above the blanket. Lucy continued on, stopping at each bed, searching in the darkness for the familiar blonde curls, her fears growing.

What if Glory hadn't kept her promise? What if she couldn't? What if . . . ?

"Luce, is that you?" a little voice suddenly called out.

"Glory!" Lucy cried softly, and she rushed toward the bed where Glory lay.

"You came!" Glory cried.

"Shh. We must be perfectly quiet. Hurry and put these on," Lucy whispered, helping Glory into her clothes. Lucy quickly put the little one's feet into her stockings and boots. Once Glory was dressed, the two tiptoed across the floor. As they neared the door, they stopped suddenly at the sound of footsteps outside in the hall. Lucy pulled Glory back against the wall, and they trembled in the shadows.

"She couldn't have gotten too far," Lucy heard someone say. "She was probably worried about her little sister."

"Rules are rules, Mistress Branch," Matron Wicks's voice snapped back. "This is just the kind of impudent behavior we cannot let go unpunished. She shall be found and punished at once."

Lucy heard the footsteps grow louder. They were coming closer. Perhaps they could hide beneath one of the beds. But any moment, Matron Wicks would be coming through the door. They would be trapped!

Lucy moved back farther into the shadows, pulling Glory with her until they found themselves backed up against a wide window ledge. Lucy turned around and placed her hand on the whitewashed pane. Hesitating for only a moment, she reached up and pulled down on the iron latch. The window swung open and a blast of cold air met her frightened face. She looked down into the darkness below.

How far was it to the ground? she wondered. How many bones would they break trying to find out? There was no time to wait for answers.

"We've got to jump," Lucy whispered to Glory as she tied the little one's shawl tightly around her. Lucy knew how terrified Glory was of heights. She also knew how much her little sister trusted her and that she would follow her anywhere.

"There's nothing else to do. It's our only chance," Lucy cried as she pulled a blanket off of an empty bed. "Are you ready?"

Though her large eyes were glassy with fear, Glory nodded as Lucy helped her up to the ledge.

"Whatever you do, you mustn't yell or scream when you jump," Lucy whispered, climbing up beside her. "I'll be right next to you."

She brought Glory's hand to her mouth and kissed it.

"One for love," Lucy said softly. "And one for luck," she added, kissing her again. Then she kissed the trembling little hand a third time. "We're going to need a lot of luck," she whispered.

It was the last thing Lucy said before they jumped.

Chapter Seven

 NCE ON THE GROUND, THE TWO SISTERS SAT dazed.

"Are you hurt?" Lucy gasped.

"I bit my lip," Glory sputtered. "And I hurt my hand."

"Here, let me see," Lucy said, taking Glory's face in her hands. "Does anything else hurt?"

Glory shook her head no.

As a cold breeze whistled in their ears, Lucy picked up the blanket, reached for Glory's hand, and quickly helped her to her feet. And they ran, as fast as they could, away from the terrible workhouse that had been their home for the last five years.

Not knowing where they were going or which way to go, the girls set out, turning first one way and then another. They had spent their entire lives following directions and walking in straight lines. Now, to have the sudden freedom to be on their own, wherever they chose, overwhelmed their senses.

The empty streets were silent, save for the sound

of their own footsteps echoing off the cobblestones. They continued to run up one street and down another, until they stopped suddenly at the sound of a loud clicking noise behind them.

Was it Matron's birch rod hitting the pavement? The thought filled Lucy with such dread that she pulled Glory into a nearby alley to hide. Lucy felt her sister's hand tightening in her own as they stepped into the shadows. Slowly, carefully, they made their way through the narrow passageway. A heap of rags against a wall suddenly stirred! Lucy was more startled when it began to speak! It was a man!

"'Ere now, wot are you two tykes up to?" the gravelly voice croaked.

"I'm afraid, Luce," Glory whimpered.

Lucy squeezed Glory's hand tighter and the two girls quickened their steps. With her free hand, Lucy fumbled for the scissors in her apron pocket. Suddenly, the man's bony fingers curled like a claw and reached out of the shadows. When Lucy felt his nails graze her cheek, she and Glory ran.

They had heard stories of the vile characters that roamed the city at night. They had heard how children were kidnapped and sold as chimney sweeps. Lucy tried not to dwell on these stories now, as she pulled Glory through the darkness.

On reaching the street, Lucy breathed a sigh of relief. She could feel that the cut on her cheek was not deep and she quickly wiped off the blood with the end of her shawl. They had gotten free of the sinister figure in the alley, with only a scratch.

Then it began to drizzle. The cold drops that splashed their faces startled them. For all the years they'd lived at Grimstone, they'd never been out in the rain. They stared at the darkened sky as if they were witnessing a miracle. Opening her mouth wide, Lucy tried to catch a drop on her tongue. Glory did the same. But their curiosity was short-lived, for the wind had whipped up and their thin rags did little to protect them from the downpour and the bitter night air. They ducked under a shop's awning to wait out the shower.

"I want to go to bed," Glory cried as she clung, shivering, to Lucy's skirts.

"We've got to keep going," Lucy said as she wrapped the blanket around Glory's shoulders. "We mustn't get caught. We can never go back."

Fearfully, Lucy looked down the street full of houses and shops. She knew that while they lived at Grimstone they could at least depend on a roof over their heads to protect them from the weather. And there was always a bowl of soup to keep them from starving. Now, suddenly, there was nowhere to turn for food and shelter.

Once the shower had stopped, they continued down the street. After a long walk, Glory began to cough and complain.

"Couldn't we stop now?" she pleaded. "My toes are all pinched and they hurt."

Lucy's feet hurt as well, for their boots were ill fitted and badly made. But where could they go? She winced at the sound of Glory's cough.

As her eyes traveled from one house to the next, Lucy thought of all the warm hearths that must be behind the many closed doors. If only there was a way to get inside and find a warm place to stay until morning.

Gathering her courage, she pulled Glory up a set of brick steps to a large wooden door. But when she tried to turn the brass doorknob, the door was locked tight. With Glory still in tow, Lucy hurried on to the next house. There she tried her hand at a window, but it was locked as well. Finally, she thought about using the brass knocker, to wake someone and try begging for shelter, but alas, her fear of being sent back overcame her. And she finally decided they would sleep under a covered doorstep.

The two climbed the few steps and fell together on the cold brick stoop. Lucy hoped the short slate roof overhead would protect them a bit from the frost. She picked up a crumpled penny paper from the stoop and smoothed it out with her hands. Then she folded it in half and tucked it under Glory's shawl to cover her chest. Together they huddled under the blanket, shivering in a fitful sleep in each other's arms until dawn.

Lucy awoke to the sound of someone calling to them from the footpath.

"Wake up, you ragamuffins!"

But Lucy was so tired and stiff from the cold, she didn't budge.

"Wake up, I tell you," she heard the deep voice cry. "The Constable is coming down the street and if he finds you laid out as you are on gentlefolks' doorsteps, you'll be marched off to Newgate, you will!"

Lucy's eyes opened wide on hearing the word "Newgate." She had heard enough stories in the workhouse about that dreaded prison. Looking up, she found herself staring at a hefty old washerwoman with a great red cabbage of a nose and a black patch over one eye. The woman's long white apron fell below her shawl and she carried a willow basket full of dirty laundry on her back. The smell of stale kippers and sour milk hung about her basket.

"Come now, dearies, you don't want to be sleeping on the prison bricks tonight, do you now?"

"No," Lucy mumbled.

"Well, it's that suit there ye'll need to stay clear of," the woman said in a husky whisper, pointing a large reddened finger down the street. "That and the stick he carries."

When Lucy spotted the man in the blue uniform talking to a crossing sweeper, she grew worried.

"Wake up, Glory," Lucy said, tugging on Glory's sleeve. "We've got to hurry."

Glory opened her eyes sleepily and tried to talk, but fell into a fit of coughing instead.

The washerwoman turned her good eye on Glory. "Here now, wot's the matter with 'er?"

Lucy put her arm around Glory. "She's a bit tired, is all," Lucy said.

"And 'alf frozen, too, I'll warrant. 'Ere now, I 'ave something for the little one's hands." Lucy watched as the woman reached into one of her pockets and pulled out a large woolen glove.

"I've been carrying it around with me for a fortnight," the washerwoman said, handing it to Lucy. "Found it on the street, outside a gin house, I did. 'Tis plain 'twas knit for a man of some size, but looking at this little one's tiny fingers, I'd say she can fit both her hands in jest fine."

Glory quickly slipped her reddened hands into the huge glove.

"We're much obliged," Lucy said to the woman.

"I only wish I had a roof of me own to offer you," the washerwoman sighed. "But I'm down on me luck meself, you see."

Lucy felt her heart warming to the woman's kindness.

"'Tis a cruel city, this," the washerwoman continued. "You best move on now, dearies. Can't stay still in this frosty air, bless my soul, you can't. You've got to stay warm, especially with the likes of the sickness going round. I've seen little ones wot were running about on a Monday and come Tuesday they be lying under the grave-digger's shovel."

Lucy shuddered at this remark. "But where can we go?" she asked.

"Why don't you try your luck down by the river?" the washerwoman suggested. "The mud-larkers have a good fire going most days."

"Mud-larkers?" repeated Lucy.

"Aye, those that be wading through the muck, looking through the trash. They're called mud-larkers."

"'Tis awfully cold to be wading in the mud," Lucy said with a shiver.

"Not by the steam factory it ain't," the woman told her. "There the mud is kept warmed all year long from the pipes running into the river."

"But what do they find in the mud?" Lucy asked.

"Oh, me!" the washerwoman clucked. "What don't they find? 'Tis all manner of things that ends up in the city's trash. And sometimes there's even treasures to be found, if you're lucky."

"Treasures?" Glory spoke up, her blue eyes widening.

The washerwoman lowered her voice. "Why, it was only last week a larker found a good china plate all in one piece, with nary a crack. And another one wot found herself a lady's hair comb with all its teeth."

Lucy gasped in surprise.

"Of course, you don't find such treasures every day," the washerwoman quickly added. "But there are plenty of nails to be found on account of all the ship-building along the river and a handful of good copper nails could fetch you half a loaf."

"How do we find the mud-larkers?" Lucy asked.

"Just follow this street 'ere," the woman said, pointing. "And turn right at the corner. 'Twill take you past Grimble's Tannery and the steam factory. The river is just below that. You'll see the mud-larkers' fires. Well, I best be off. Good luck to you, dearies," she said with a wave, and adjusted the large basket on her back.

Lucy felt a pang of longing as she watched the kindhearted woman walk away. If only she and Glory could go with her. If only they had someone as strong and kindly as the washerwoman to show them the way. But it was a momentary wish. For Lucy had learned early on in her life that she was to be the only one they could depend on. And she knew that somehow it was up to her to find the courage to see them through this dangerous turn their lives had taken.

Chapter Eight

OME NOW, GLORY," LUCY SAID AS SHE helped her sister to her feet. "Let's go to the river and see what we find."

"Do you suppose we'll find a treasure?" Glory asked weakly.

"I don't know. But if we can just find enough nails to buy us a crust of bread 'twill be treasure enough."

Glory nodded. "My stomach hurts ever so much. I'm so hungry."

"I know," Lucy said, feeling the familiar tug of pain in her own empty stomach. "I know."

When she saw another crumpled paper in the gutter, Lucy quickly reached for it. The smell of a meat pie was still in it and the sisters took turns licking the grease from the paper. But the scent of the meat and the taste of grease on their tongues only served to heighten their hunger, leaving their mouths watering for more.

Together they headed down the footpath, following the washerwoman's directions. The sounds of life on the streets grew to a din.

Carts and coaches rattled over cobblestones, while crossing sweepers shouted directions, and street vendors hawked their wares. The city's early morning commotion was exciting. But the biting cold and the hunger that gnawed at their empty bellies kept them moving forward.

After the drab, colorless life in the workhouse, the jumble of brightly colored objects lining the busy street was a startling sight. The street vendors selling tea, tallow, cigars, rat poison, sugary confections, and more, that clamored to be heard were like nothing they'd ever seen. But most enticing of all was the sound of a bell ringing, and the muffin man's cry: "Who'll buy a crumpet for a halfpenny?"

He wore a blue and white waistcoat and a white neckerchief round his neck. A large wooden platter sat atop his head. Piled high on the tray was a mountain of crumpets. Never had the girls seen so much food at once. Taking Glory's arm, Lucy hurried forward.

As they approached the muffin man, the aroma of his freshly baked breads was so overpowering that both girls stopped and stared.

"Fresh crumpets 'ere, still warm from the baker's oven," the man called out in a high-pitched voice.

Lucy had never begged for food before, and she wasn't sure how to do it.

"I'm ever so hungry, Luce," Glory's faint voice reached her ears now, as the smell of cinnamon and sweet dough filled the air. The bowl of watery soup the two had eaten the day before did little to appease their gnawing hunger.

"Please, sir," Lucy cried out piteously. "Could you find it in your heart to spare something for a poor, unfortunate pair of orphans?"

"I could find lots in me 'art, if you could find the coin to pay me," the man snapped back at her. "Push off now, for you're keeping away the good trade." He waved a long white-gloved hand and Lucy took a step back.

If only we had something good to trade, thought Lucy. It was then that she remembered the scissors she had in her pocket.

"Begging your pardon, sir," she said, pulling them from her pocket. "Would these do, instead of a coin?"

The muffin man's eyes widened, and before she could say another word he swooped up the scissors and reached for two large crumpets atop his plate. Lucy quickly shoved them into her pocket.

"Thank you kindly," she said. "And could you tell me, sir, is Grimble's Tannery close by?"

"You need only to follow this," the muffin man said, bringing a long gloved finger to his nose. "Keep to this street and then turn at the corner, there. And don't worry. You'll know you're close by the smell."

Lucy thanked the man again and with Glory at her side, the two continued down the footpath. When they passed a skeleton of a woman in ragged garments standing with her hand out, Glory pulled on Lucy's skirt.

"She looks so horribly thin, Luce. Couldn't we give her some of our crumpet?" Glory pleaded.

"No," Lucy said firmly. "We can't be giving away what little we have."

But Glory's face was so sorrowful, Lucy knew she could not refuse her. Instead, she reached into her pocket and broke off a piece of one of the crumpets.

"God bless your kindness," the woman whispered as Lucy placed it in her outstretched hand.

As hungry as she was, Lucy waited until they got free of the crowd that had overtaken the footpath before pulling the crumpets out. Living as long as she had in the workhouse, she feared someone would try to grab them from her hand. As they walked away from the crowd, a new scent met their noses.

"Chestnuts, 'ere, roasted to perfection . . . ," a vendor cried out as he stood beside his cart. Lucy saw that the cart was filled with chestnuts roasting over a good little fire. As the vendor was busy talking to a customer, Lucy and Glory were able to inch close enough to the fire to warm themselves.

Lucy quickly took the crumpets from her pocket and offered Glory one. A hungry-eyed boy, wearing a large tattered coat and a paper hat on his head, called to them from a stoop.

"'Ere now, how'd you come by them crumpets?" he demanded. "Did you pinch them?"

Lucy glared over the piece that she was stuffing into her mouth. When she had swallowed her last bit of crumbs, she licked her lips contentedly. Never in all her years at the workhouse had she tasted anything so delicious.

"I didn't pinch it," she finally answered. "'Twas a fair trade."

"Wot for?" the boy called. "Wot did you trade for?"

"For a pair of scissors," Glory spoke up.

"Did they work?" the boy asked.

"Yes, they worked rather well," Lucy sniffed, for she did not like the boy's tone.

"And you only got two crumpets for a working pair of scissors?" The boy sighed, with a roll of his eyes. "Why, they would be worth a whole plate of crumpets, you ninny. Are you from the country, that you could be so duped?"

"We're from the work . . . ," Glory began to answer, but Lucy was quick to clap her hand over Glory's mouth.

"'Tis no business of yours where we're from," she said defiantly, her face burning with shame. If only she had stopped to think about the scissors' worth! How could she have been so stupid! She could have traded them for so much more! How would they ever survive if she made mistakes like that?

Lucy grabbed hold of Glory's hand now and pulled her away.

"Luce, why did that boy call you a ninny?" Glory asked as they hurried down the footpath behind a woman carrying a bucket of oysters on her head.

"Because I am a ninny, that's why," Lucy muttered, kicking a clod of frozen horse manure at her feet. She closed her eyes as she tried to fight back her sudden tears.

"We've no money for food and no place to sleep. How are we to manage if I keep making such big mistakes? Oh, Glory, 'tis your bad luck to have such a ninny for a sister."

The seriousness of their situation suddenly weighed so heavily on Lucy that she sank down on the curb in despair. As she buried her head in her hands, she felt a tug on her skirt and a hand on her shoulder. When she lifted her head she saw Glory's anxious face beside her.

"You're not a ninny, Luce," the little one whispered. "'Tis not bad luck to have you for a sister at all. 'Tis good luck, I'd say. 'Tis the best of luck."

At the sound of Glory's soft voice and the feel of her gentle touch, Lucy felt herself smiling in spite of her worries. No matter how dark things seemed, Glory's bright spirit always shone through.

Lucy brushed the tears from her eyes with the back of her hand. Then she took the edge of her skirt and wiped Glory's runny nose.

"All right, then," she said, taking hold of the little one's hand. "Let's see how much luck we have at the river."

Together the two headed down the footpath toward the Thames. Along the way they talked of the treasure they hoped to find there, of ladies' hair combs and china plates "with nary a crack."

CHAPTER NINE

 HE AIR NEAR THE TANNERY WAS HEAVY WITH chimney smoke and in some places it was so thick it seemed to swallow up the street and all the buildings that surrounded it. Glory's cough worsened and Lucy's eyes began to water from the smoke. She stopped to tighten Glory's shawl around her chest.

"Oh, no, no, Luce! What's that nasty smell?" Glory asked, pulling her shawl over her face.

The stench was so bad it nearly took Lucy's breath away and she, too, lifted her own shawl over her nose. Never had they smelled anything so foul.

They looked out over the dark water to the boats that were moored at the docks. Neither girl had ever seen a river before, and despite the bad smell, they stood staring, awed by the sight of it. A number of small fires were burning on the shore.

They made their way down the rickety set of wooden stairs that led to the river's edge. There they hiked up their skirts and took off their stockings and boots, and they headed for a fire that was burning a short distance away. The horrid odor of hides and decaying horseflesh hung heavy in the dense air.

At the caw of a blackbird, both girls looked up and followed the bird's flight down the length of the shoreline. There, stooping in the mud, were dozens of poor, ragged children and withered old women.

As she looked over at Glory, Lucy was struck by just how desperate their situation had become. The little one's legs stuck out from beneath her hiked-up skirts like two spindly twigs. Her ankles were like two reddened knobs above her tiny muddied feet. If Glory were to grow any thinner, or if her cold were to grow any worse, she surely would not survive.

As the girls approached a ragtag group of mud-larkers warming their hands before a burning log, Lucy listened desperately to hear talk of treasure and where the best place to look for it might be. But there was little conversation among the dirty-faced children and adults who stood rubbing their filthy hands over the flames. Their unwelcoming silence kept Lucy from speaking to them. She and Glory had to squeeze their way into a huddle of bodies to reach the fire, and even then they were too far from it to feel much warmth.

"Shove off," a man said, elbowing them further away.

Lucy took Glory's hand, and as the two stepped closer to the river's edge the wet muck clung to their skin, covering their feet and oozing up their legs.

"I shan't be able to put my hands in it," Glory whimpered as she eyed the dark sludge uneasily. "It smells so evil."

"'Tisn't so bad," Lucy whispered. "Why look, there's rope! We could sell that if it's a long enough piece." She was about to reach for it, when a wild-eyed woman came up beside her and snatched it away.

"Wot's this, then?" the woman muttered, giving the rope a tug. To her horror, she discovered that the rope she was holding was not a rope at all, but a tail. And attached to the tail was a large river rat that scrambled frantically in midair, thrashing to get away.

As the rat turned its head back toward the woman, it curled back its lips and gnashed its pointed teeth. The woman gave out a loud scream and released her hand. She stumbled backward, nearly knocking Lucy down as the rat quickly disappeared back into the mud.

Other larkers looked up and laughed. "At least he didn't bite off your hand, Mol," one man called.

"Remember poor little Charlie wot lost half his finger?" another said. "Bit clean off by a river rat."

"You never know what you're going to find," an old woman cackled. "Why, just yesterday I was larking down by the Crabtree Wharf and I pulled out a skull. A human skull 'twas, too. Put me fingers right through the holes where the eyes had once been."

As the larkers continued to trade horror stories, Lucy and Glory moved away from the group.

"Let's try over there," Lucy said, pointing down the shoreline.

"Oh, mercy!" Glory cried, clenching her tiny fists. "I shan't be able to put my hands in the mud, not if there are rats and skulls waiting there."

Lucy frowned. The encounter with the rat had shaken them both badly. But as she listened to Glory cough, Lucy thought about what the rest of the day could bring with no food and no money for lodgings. Glory's cold was sure to grow worse if they had to spend another night sleeping out in the cold. She had no choice. She would have to return to the mud.

Lucy rolled her sleeves up to her elbows and looked back down at the muck. She took a deep breath and thrust her arm into the thick ooze.

The two sisters soon discovered that the business of mud-larking proved a harsh way to earn a crust of bread. An hour later found them still stooped over the putrid muck. Glory could not be persuaded to put her hands into it. So it was left to Lucy to hunt. The only treasure she'd managed to find was a handful of bones and eight bent nails.

"Couldn't we go back to the street?" Glory pleaded, her blue eyes watering from the wind. "There was such a lovely fire by the chestnut cart. And it smelled ever so much better than this."

"It's no good for us to go smelling chestnuts roasting if we haven't the coin to buy any," Lucy pointed out. "We've got to find something here or we'll not be having anything to eat tonight. All we need is to find one good thing." She sighed.

"But all I see is mud," complained Glory. "I don't see any plates or combs or any treasure at all. Just mud, ever so much mud . . ."

As Lucy's eyes slowly traveled back and forth over the muck she stopped suddenly and stared.

"What's that sticking up there?" she whispered, pointing down beside Glory's foot.

"Where!" shrieked Glory, shutting her eyes tight.

"There, look down by your foot."

"I can't," Glory whimpered, her eyes still closed.

"Move over then, so I can see," Lucy said.

Without opening her eyes, Glory took a step backward.

"What is it, Luce?" she whispered after a moment of silence. "Is it a rat's tail? Is it a skull?"

Lucy plunged her hand down into the mud. As she did, her fingertips grazed something hard. Holding her breath, she lunged forward and grabbed on to the stiff form that was sticking in the muck. Her fingers ran over the object as she frantically tried to identify it.

"Have mercy on my soul!" Lucy gasped. For as she lifted the form from the mud and saw what she was holding, she shuddered. It was a hand! A tiny stiffened hand!

"A baby!" Glory gasped. "Is it a baby?"

Lucy instantly let go, and the rigid form splashed back onto the sludge. They could see the shape of the head, but it was so covered in mud that the only recognizable feature was the left eye. Both girls trembled as it stared up at them, bright blue and unblinking.

"'Tisn't a baby at all," Lucy whispered excitedly as she wiped the mud from the tiny face. "Why, we've found ourselves a doll, Glory! We've found ourselves a doll!"

Chapter Ten

EVER HAVING OWNED ANYTHING AS LUX-
urious as a doll, the two sisters were
mesmerized by the soggy, mud-covered
figure. Lucy lifted the little doll from the muck. She
could see that the cloth body was ruined. There was
neither dress, nor hat, and though the face was worn,
it still held a beautiful smile. It was the smile that
struck Lucy immediately, for it curved up ever so
slightly, causing the doll to look as if she knew a secret, a happy secret.

"Why, just look at her cheeks," whispered Lucy, as
she spit on the doll's face and rubbed it clean with the
end of her shawl. "Did you ever see a lovelier pink?
And see how clear her eyes are, with such fine long
lashes, painted as perfect as you please."

"Oh, Luce, might I hold her?" begged Glory.

"She's much too muddy," Lucy pointed out. "But I
suppose we could give her a bath."

So they walked up to the water's edge and dunked
the doll in, squeezing out as much of the dirty water

from her cloth body as they could. When she was quite wrung out, Lucy gave her a sniff and made a face.

"She's still got a nasty smell about her, and it will be a long while before she's dried out."

But Glory paid no mind to this complaint. She reached under her shawl and pulled out the folded paper Lucy had put there. Glory quickly unfolded the paper and held it out as if it were a blanket to receive a baby. Lucy gently placed the dirty doll into Glory's waiting arms. The little girl's hands trembled nervously, as she reached for the precious treasure. And as Lucy watched, a broad smile broke over Glory's face. Her eyes brightened and her face shone with pleasure. Lucy had never seen her look so happy.

"Oh, Luce," Glory whispered, holding the doll in her arms. "It's her, Luce. It's her! It's Morning Glory! We found her just as you said we would!"

Lucy was so glad to see Glory's utter joy that she didn't have the heart to tell her that she couldn't keep the doll. A toy was a luxury they could ill afford. Perhaps this doll would fetch them enough for a good hot meal. Lucy would soon have to tell Glory that the doll must be sold. But she wanted to give her a few more moments of pleasure.

Lucy found a piece of dirty rag on the ground and used it to wipe the mud from their feet. They quickly got back into their stockings and boots. Once they reached the dock, the dank smell of the river was replaced by the sharp scent of fresh tar in the air. Lucy wrinkled her nose at the pungent tang of tobacco and the heavy fumes from the barrels of rum that lined the quay.

Back on the street, they found the footpaths so narrow that they had to carefully maneuver their way around the piles of horse manure and broken crockery that littered the street.

Lucy reached for Glory's arm at the sight of the hard-bitten sailors' faces and the great muscled giants that loaded the ships. As they hurried past the shops displaying rope and sailcloth in their windows, Lucy watched Glory with the doll. How would she ever be able to take her away?

"You must have been quite beautiful once, before you ended up in the mud," she heard Glory tell the doll. "You were waiting there just for me, just the way my sister said you would. And now we'll never have to be apart again."

Lucy bit down nervously on her lip as she listened. She knew she had to tell Glory the truth, for it would be too cruel to let her go on thinking that the doll was hers to keep.

"Glory," Lucy interrupted. "Could it be that you're wrong? Maybe you've made a mistake."

Glory frowned. "A mistake?"

"About the doll," Lucy said gently. "Maybe she's not your Morning Glory, after all. Maybe she's someone else's doll."

"Oh, no," Glory said firmly, as she stopped to stroke the doll's head. "This is my Morning Glory, I can tell."

"How?" Lucy asked. "How can you tell?"

The little girl's face brightened. "Why, just look at her smile. See how it curves up at the side? Just as you always said."

Lucy looked at the doll's face, and once again she was struck by the mysterious smile.

"Yes, but Glory . . . ," Lucy began.

"And 'tis just as you always said at the end of the story," Glory interrupted. "You said that my heart would know her when I saw her. And it does. It's her! It's her! I know it's her!"

Lucy was speechless. She wanted to tell her sister that it was all only a make-believe story, that orphan girls were never meant to own anything as grand as dolls, and that all the promises Lucy had made were as empty as their threadbare pockets.

But try as she might, the words wouldn't come. Lucy could only watch in silence as Glory smiled lovingly at the dirty old doll she held tightly in her arms.

Chapter Eleven

HE TWO SISTERS TRUDGED UP AND DOWN the dock, trying to trade the little they'd found. But the sellers of sailcloth and rum were not interested in bones and nails and neither were the tobacco shops they entered.

When they finally happened on a little cobwebby shop full of rags and baskets of bones, Lucy guided Glory up to the door.

"Wot 'ave you brought me, then," a voice called to them as they stepped inside. A strong musty smell mixed with lye hung in the dingy airless room. Lines dripping with strips of wet rags were strung from one end of the shop to the other, while piles of colored cloth covered the floor.

Lucy followed the voice under the dripping canopy, through the maze of rag piles, to the back of the shop, where a heavyset redheaded woman dressed in a green gown and a tattered velvet bonnet stood behind a counter. With a chubby hand, the woman waved them toward her.

Lucy and Glory stepped forward, and as they did, the warmth of a coal fire washed over them. Lucy sighed with relief, unclenching her frozen fingers. But when she laid down the few bones and the handful of nails on the wooden counter the woman offered only a small packet of rags in return.

"Will you give no more than this?" Lucy asked, disappointed with such a meager offering.

"Seeing how thin your shawls be, you should be glad I'm giving you that much," the woman snorted. "These nails you've brought are bent and the bones are few." She pointed to the small packet on the counter. "And my name's not Florrie Nuggins if them's not clean rags of good quality I'll be giving in return. Looks to me like you could use some extra padding against the weather." She leaned over the counter to look at Glory, who had begun to cough.

"Tsk, tsk, ducks," Florrie Nuggins clucked. "Did you catch a chill at the river? Go on, and 'ave a sit by the fire and warm yourself. Go on, then." She pointed to the bench before the stove, and Glory did as she was told. Glory was so tired and the fire felt so warm, that no sooner had she sat down than she closed her eyes and fell sound asleep.

"Are you sleeping out in the weather? Is that where she come by that nasty cough? Are you all on your own then?" the woman asked.

"We're getting by," Lucy said vaguely.

"Well, you'd best find some warm place for her tonight or you could lose her. They found a girl wot froze to death, sleeping outside just last week. Do you remember that wicked cold night?" The woman clicked her tongue and shook her head. "Mercy, she's fallen asleep as we speak."

As gently as she could, Lucy lifted the old doll from her sister's arms and carried her over to the counter. Though she hated to do it, she knew what she had to do.

"Would you buy this doll?" Lucy whispered. "We found her down at the river."

But Florrie Nuggins shook her head no. "I stick to rags and bones. It's wot I know best. Why don't you take her over to Thimblebee's. I daresay she's a sorry sight, though her head is right pretty. Miss Thimble-bee might be interested in her head."

"Miss Thimblebee?" Lucy repeated.

"Of Thimblebee's Doll Shop," Florrie Nuggins said, nodding toward the door. "'Tis the little build-ing at the end of Mulberry Lane. Just follow the al-ley."

Lucy looked back at her sleeping sister.

"The little one can rest 'ere while you're at Thim-blebee's, if you like," Florrie Nuggins offered.

Lucy wondered what she should do. She had

never left her sister with a stranger before. But seeing Glory so warm and content, Lucy decided that the rest by the fire would do her more good than dragging her through the cold.

"But you can't walk into Thimblebee's wearing those dirty rags," Florrie Nuggins said. "Miss Thimblebee is right particular about her dolls. Won't have any grime in her shop."

Lucy looked down to see her mud-stained apron and filthy skirt. She looked over at Glory sound asleep in front of the fire. Glory's apron, though dirty, was cleaner than Lucy's.

And if I turn it inside out, Lucy thought, *'twill look cleaner still.*

She quickly untied her own apron and left it on the bench beside Glory. Then she reached behind her sister and silently untied her apron strings. Once she had the apron in her hands Lucy went back to the counter and picked up the old doll.

She felt a pang of sorrow as she thought about the little one waking to find her Morning Glory gone. But Lucy knew that there was nothing else for them to do. If they were going to survive in the city, they would have to sell something and the doll was all they had.

"Go on, then, if you're going," Mistress Nuggins called. "And take care not to tarry, for me Mister will be back soon from his stall on Pettycoat Lane, and he don't take kindly to no riffraff hanging about."

"I shan't be long," Lucy assured the shopkeeper. "I shan't be long," she whispered to Glory as she kissed the top of her head.

And so with Glory's apron tied round her waist and Morning Glory in her arms, Lucy hurried out of the door. Meanwhile, in the musty old shop, amidst the lines of drying rags and piles of bones, little Glory Wolcott slept on, unaware that the doll she had dreamt of all her life had been taken from her arms.

CHAPTER TWELVE

OLLOWING FLORRIE NUGGINS'S DIRECTIONS, Lucy made her way to Number Nine Mulberry Lane. There she found a quirky-looking little bit of a building. The miniature structure had a fanciful air about it, with its crooked chimney that tilted toward the Thames and its peaks and spires that rose up above the crumbling old roof tiles. Six blackbirds perched on the highest peak.

Window boxes overflowed with a seasonal display of holly, berries, and pinecones. A large black lantern hung beside a plum-colored door. Above the lantern was a wooden sign.

Lucy could not read the letters on the sign, but she felt her heart stop at the sight of the figure that was painted below them. For it was the figure of a doll, a lovely, smiling doll. Lucy's chilled fingers tightened around Morning Glory as she peered into Thimblebee's large display window.

Never in all her life had Lucy imagined such splendor, such beauty! For there in the window were dolls in striped satin balancing on wires and dolls with straw bonnets and baskets of flowers. There were miniature lady dolls looking most prim and proper and fancy wax dolls in frilly dresses with fine crystal necklaces. Sweet-faced baby dolls slept in their cradles, while golden-haired porcelain dolls took their tea at a little table.

Lucy looked down anxiously at Morning Glory in her arms. Suddenly the doll's dirty, stained body and worn face seemed pitiful compared to the beautiful dolls in the window. It took all of her courage to climb the three brick steps and push the plum door open. As she did, bells sounded cheerily above her head.

"Surely I'm dreaming," Lucy whispered, stepping into the cozy confines of Thimblebee's display room. Her eyes traveled over the lace-lined shelves from one glorious doll to the next. Without thinking she reached out to touch a doll's blue velvet slipper.

But the sight of her filthy fingers, her nails caked with grime, beside such pristine beauty was so startling that she thrust her hand behind her back. Looking down at her ragged skirt, so frayed and full of stains, and her old worn boots, cracked and covered with mud, Lucy felt her cheeks burn with shame.

When she looked up she saw a round-faced little hen of a woman rushing toward her. The woman was dressed in a blue velveteen frock with a lace collar and cuffs. A bit of white lace was also pinned just above her silver bun. With her button of a nose and her cheeks that glowed rose-pink, she seemed almost doll-like herself.

"What poor heap of rags is this? We mustn't have any begging here," the old woman cried, on seeing Lucy. "You must leave at once."

"Excuse me, mum, but I've not come to beg," Lucy said, taking a small step toward the counter. "I've come to speak to Miss Thimblebee."

"And so you are," the old woman replied.

Lucy tried to steady her voice. "I've come to sell you a doll," she said.

Miss Thimblebee peered over her spectacles at the filthy little figure in Lucy's hands. "Oh, my stars!" she gasped.

"I found her in the mud beside the river," Lucy told her.

Miss Thimblebee tapped on the counter with her thimbled finger, and Lucy carefully laid Morning Glory down.

"Quite ruined," the old woman muttered. "But the head is interesting, and in tolerable condition. Good clear eyes. And she has a look about her. There's something about her smile, quite unusual. Found her in the mud, did you?"

"Yes, upon my mother's grave, I swear 'tis the truth," Lucy said, shaking her head.

"'Tis most ungodly to swear on your mother's grave," Miss Thimblebee scolded. "And as for this doll, she's in such sorry condition . . ."

"Oh, please! I'm so hungry!" Lucy cried. "I don't know what I shall do if you won't buy her."

The old woman's face seemed to soften. She turned Morning Glory over in her wrinkled hands and then laid her back on the counter. "A penny," she declared. "I shall give you a penny." And without another word she whisked the old doll from the counter and laid down a shiny penny in its place.

"A penny!" Lucy cried. With trembling fingers she reached for the coin and examined it closely. It was the first and only money she had ever held in her entire life.

"Here now, what's that on the hem of your apron?" Miss Thimblebee squinted over her spectacles as she pointed to the little gray blossom.

"'Tis a morning glory," Lucy answered in a small voice.

"Indeed," the old woman murmured, as she beckoned Lucy to step closer. "And who, pray tell, embroidered this glorious morning glory?"

Lucy stared dumbly at the blossom, fearful of why

she was being questioned. Did the woman think she had stolen the thread?

"Speak up, my girl," Miss Thimblebee ordered.

Lucy took a deep breath and closed her eyes. "'Twas me, mum," she said softly. "I stitched the flower."

"Remarkable!" The old woman sighed. "'Tis a gift, indeed, to be able to embroider with such skill."

Lucy was unused to compliments; no one had ever complimented her work before. She didn't know how to answer. Before she could, the paisley curtain behind the counter suddenly parted and a tall, thin woman wearing a white mobcap and apron to match burst through. She had a tape measure around her neck and on her wrist she wore a cushion full of pins.

"Oh, Miss Thimblebee!" the woman cried out. "I've terrible news!"

"What is it, Bess?" the old woman asked.

"'Tis young Mary, mum. She won't be coming back this year, that's sure. Her fever was so high, they didn't think she'd make it through the night."

Miss Thimblebee looked stricken. "Without our Hearts Girl, we shan't be able to finish another doll!"

"'Tis so, mum," Bess agreed. "And with Christmas but two weeks away, how will we ever fill all our orders? Wouldn't it do for one of us to give the dolls their hearts, mum? And I being the head doll-maker, well, I thought I might try."

Miss Thimblebee clutched her chest.

"Oh, no, Bess, that will never do! For it has long been a tradition at Thimblebee's that only a girl can give the dolls their hearts. And only a special girl, with a special gift, can do it. A Thimblebee's doll is not a Thimblebee's doll unless it has the proper heart."

"But where are we to find such a girl in so little time?" Bess lamented. "And if we don't fill our Christmas orders . . ." Her voice trailed off.

"If we don't fill our Christmas orders, Thimblebee's reputation could be ruined. . . ." Miss Thimblebee finished the sentence in a shaky whisper. There was a moment of silence as the two women stood wringing their hands.

Lucy moved toward the door, deciding it best if she left before either one of them burst into tears. But no sooner had she taken a step back than the old woman took a step toward her. Lucy could see that a gleam had suddenly come into Miss Thimblebee's eyes.

And before Lucy could leave, the wrinkled old hand reached out for her apron once more. "What is your name, child? And where did you say you came from?"

Chapter Thirteen

UCY FELT HER THROAT TIGHTEN. WOULD the woman send her back to Grimstone? Should she tell the old woman the truth? "I'm Lucy. Lucy Wolcott," she whispered hoarsely. "And I live on the streets, mum."

A long silence followed as Miss Thimblebee continued to stare. Her gaze was so deep that Lucy felt she could see clear into her heart. And when a flicker of a smile crossed the old woman's face, Lucy let out a sigh of relief.

"Bess, fetch a clean pinafore and have Emma set a pot of water on the stove," Miss Thimblebee ordered. "We'll need to scrub off some of that grime before we can put her to the test."

Bess gasped. "Oh, goodness, no, mum! You can't possibly be thinking this girl . . ."

"'Tis exactly the girl that I'm thinking of, my dear Bess," Miss Thimblebee explained, taking up the hem of Glory's apron in her hand. "These stitches are extraordinary. 'Tis plain to see that the seamstress of this blossom has great talent. Once we scrub the child's hands and give her needle and thread, we'll see if she is indeed the one who stitched this flower. And if she is, then we have found the very girl we're looking for."

"But mum!" cried Bess. "You can't mean that. . . ."

"Oh, but I do," Miss Thimblebee replied as she turned to look back at Lucy. "Miss Lucy Wolcott," she said, "I do believe the angels have sent you to me this Christmas season. And now we shall see if you prove me right."

Dazed, Lucy was hurried through the paisley curtains, into the back room. There a basin was filled with warm water, her hands were scrubbed clean and dried, and she was given a clean flannel pinafore to put over her dirty clothes.

"Sit, then, until Miss Thimblebee is finished waiting on her customers up front," Bess ordered. She guided Lucy to a little bench beside the fire. Lucy sat and stared at two young women who were bent over a long worktable. Their heads bobbed up in unison at the sound of Bess's voice.

"Come, girls," Bess called. "Emma, fetch a cup of tea. Iris, reach into the biscuit box and fetch us a scone."

Soon a cup of hot tea was set on the bench and a scone was placed in Lucy's hand. Too surprised to speak, Lucy tried to steady her trembling fingers as she broke off a large piece of the pastry. She quickly hid it in her pocket to save for Glory.

"Oh, mercy. I think I've died and gone to heaven," Lucy murmured as she took a sip of tea. For the warmth of the stove, the buttery scone, the hot tea, and the smell of clean cloth all made her senses sing with pleasure. Adding to her delight was this secret peek into the doll shop's workroom. For it was here, amid the clutter of ribbons and lace and beside boxes of buttons and bolts of soft silk, that the doll-makers worked their magic.

As Lucy silently looked on, the women returned to their places at the long wooden table. In a flurry of ripping and snipping, with thimbled fingers flying, Lucy listened to the three whispering, gently coaxing their creations to life, while up front the cheery ring of bells ushered in one customer after another through the shop's plum-colored door. For it was the Christmas season, and Thimblebee's busiest time.

When Miss Thimblebee did finally join them, she was quick to announce her intention to give Lucy the test that would determine her skills.

"If you have the talent, then you shall have the job for this Christmas season. A place to sleep by the fire and your meals will be your pay. Will that suit you, child?"

Lucy swallowed hard at the thought of her good fortune. She was so overcome with joy that she could only manage to nod her head.

"Splendid!" Miss Thimblebee beamed, as she directed Lucy to the highest stool at the worktable. Bess brought the needle tray and Emma pulled some cards of embroidery thread from a large basket. Iris set a newly made doll on the worktable.

There was a sudden silence in the room as the others looked on, waiting and watching Lucy's every move. With her heart pounding, Lucy stared down at the smiling doll. And suddenly she saw another face staring back at her, one pinched and worn from exhaustion and cold. It was Glory's face that she saw in that doll. And when she closed her eyes and placed her hand on the doll's smooth chest, it was her sister's own heart that she was imagining.

With the warmth of the fire at her back and the sweet taste of the scone still in her mouth, Lucy thought about how both their lives could change in one moment, if only she could give Miss Thimblebee what she wanted!

She opened her eyes and picked up a card of the darkest red floss. With trembling fingers she guided the thread through the eye of the needle.

Slowly, silently, Lucy traced a heart over the doll's chest with the tip of her finger. Emma and Iris snickered and whispered to see her attempt to make the heart without first drawing it in chalk. Bess gave Miss Thimblebee a wary look, as never so deep a red had been used on a baby doll's heart. But Miss Thimblebee only looked on in quiet anticipation.

With her eyes intent on her work, Lucy took a deep breath and pricked the clean white chest. A loud gasp could be heard, as the others leaned in closer. With each stitch she took, Lucy softly murmured to the doll, words none but the two could hear. Then, with a final stitch, she knotted her thread and buried the knot deep within the perfectly shaped heart.

And perfection it was, in color, size, shape, and form. It was clearly a heart meant for no other. A heart so sweet and dainty that Miss Thimblebee and the others were quite taken aback. At first Lucy feared they were not pleased with her work, and she was ready to offer to rip out her stitches. But before she could, Miss Thimblebee scooped up the baby doll and held it up for all to see. A hush fell over the group. No one had ever seen a heart filled with such love and tenderness.

Miss Thimblebee finally broke the silence. "Miss Lucy Wolcott, welcome to Thimblebee's!" she proclaimed. "You may begin work tonight. We will only be needing you until Christmas Eve, but it's steady work until then and heaven knows you look as if you could use it."

Lucy could hardly believe her ears.

"As a Hearts Girl you must keep the fire going," Miss Thimblebee continued. "I do so hate to think of my dolls catching a chill. Of course, you're not to let anyone in once the shop is closed and the door is locked. During the day you're to work in the window, for the customers do so love watching dolls receive their hearts.

"You may take off the pinafore and collect your things now. I'll expect you back by closing. Is that agreeable to you?"

"Oh, yes, mum," Lucy murmured, pulling the pinafore off her head. But in all the excitement she had given little thought as to what she should do about Glory. Miss Thimblebee had made it clear that no one else was allowed in the shop after closing. The promise of a warm place to sleep and food to eat was too good to be true. But Lucy knew that taking care of Glory was most important of all. What was she going to do?

As she headed back to the rag and bone shop, Lucy kept her hand in her pocket, tightly clutching the coin she had gotten for Morning Glory. Looking around, she worried that someone might discover she had something of value and try to rob her.

As the fog rolled in, a delicious smell filled the air.

"Meat pies! A penny a pie!" a vendor cried out.

A penny a pie! Why, I could buy one! Lucy marveled. But she kept the coin in her pocket. As she passed several other carts with vendors hawking warm plum duffs and ginger beers she grew light-headed with happiness and hunger. There was so much to choose from! Though she wanted desperately to buy something to eat at once, Lucy decided to wait so that Glory could choose.

She tried to imagine Glory eating a meat pie or a warm plum duff. But try as she might, Lucy could picture only one expression on Glory's face and it had nothing to do with happiness. For the only look Lucy could imagine was that of a broken heart. It was the look the little one would have when she discovered the truth, when she discovered that her sister had taken her doll to be sold.

With her own heart sinking, Lucy made her way back up Mulberry Lane.

CHAPTER FOURTEEN

HEN LUCY FINALLY RETURNED TO NUGGINS Rag and Bone Shop, the bench by the fire was empty. Instead of finding Mistress Nuggins, she found a rotund man with a bushy brown mustache and a crimson pockmarked face standing behind the counter.

"Wot do you want?" he barked on seeing Lucy.

"My sister," Lucy began. "Where is my sister?"

"That little wretch with the cough? I threw her out on her bony little duff," the man said matter-of-factly.

Lucy gasped. "But Mistress Nuggins promised . . ."

"The trouble with Mistress Nuggins," the man declared, "is that she's got a heart as big as her duff, which is by no means bony nor little. And the trouble with that is we ain't no almshouse, we ain't. Nuggins Rags and Bones, that's wot it says on the sign. Don't say nothin' about takin' in every little beggar from here to Drury Lane. So you can just push off now and don't be comin' back."

Lucy was dumbfounded.

"I said push off," the man growled.

With her heart beating wildly, Lucy headed for the door but stopped suddenly and spun back around. "Please, sir," she begged. "Can you at least tell me, did you see which way my sister went? She's only six, sir, and she's very sick, she is. And she doesn't know the city so well."

"She's gone is all I know," the man grumbled. "Likely as not she's been kidnapped and picked up by a sweep and sent up some chimney. 'Tis where all you riffraff belong, if you ask me. Out of sight, sweeping soot . . ."

But Lucy did not stay to hear more. She flung open the door and raced out to the street.

"Glory!" she called frantically. "Glory, where are you?"

But the only reply was the shout of a torch boy running ahead of a coach, his lamp swinging from his long pole to light the way. For the streets had suddenly given themselves over to the heavy breath of a winter's fog. The footpath, which moments ago had a clear view, was being swallowed up in a thick haze. "Glory!" Lucy yelled. "Glory, where are you?"

But Glory didn't answer. It was as if the little girl had vanished in the fog along with the cobbled streets and buildings. Lucy started off in one direction and then anxiously turned to try another. All the while the dampness clung to her meager clothes, seeping into her skin, right down to her bones. She shuddered to think of Glory shivering and lost in the cold.

Lucy cried as she tripped over a curb and fell to her knees. It suddenly seemed as if everything was conspiring against her, even the weather.

When she spied a lamplighter making his rounds, Lucy was seized with a new panic. Time was running out. Nightfall was approaching. The hour when thieves and low-minded criminals stepped out of the shadows was near.

All at once, the horror stories Lucy had heard at the workhouse came rushing back to her. She recalled the tales of the orphans kidnapped and sold to chimney sweeps, how their feet were pricked with pins to force them up the dark narrow chimneys. She remembered, too, the tales of children stolen while they slept in back alleys, bludgeoned for their shoes.

Lucy's stomach heaved. Her fear was so overpowering, so strong, she ached with the pain of it. How could she have trusted her sister to a stranger?

"Oh, Glory, what have I done?" Lucy cried into the wind. "What have I done?"

CHAPTER FIFTEEN

LUCY SEARCHED UP AND DOWN THE STREET, stopping everyone she passed.

"Have you seen a small girl in a gray dress and blue shawl?" she asked. But the crossing sweeper just shrugged his shoulders. A woman hawking matches from a basket did the same.

"I sees lots of little mites go up and down all day," said a dustman, who was shoveling cinders into a wagon. "They all looks alike to me."

A boy selling birds on the corner shook his head. "Can't see much in this pea souper."

"Pea souper?"

"The fog," the boy explained. "'Tis as thick as me mum's pea soup." He reached into one of his many crates and pulled out a dove.

"Wot about you, my beauty?" he whispered to the bird in his hands. "'Ave you seen the little girl?"

As desperate as Lucy was, she knew better than to think a dove could speak, though she waited, just the same. But the small bird was silent, its gray feathers fluttering against the boy's dirty fingers.

Lucy turned and walked away. The street grew deserted as the weather turned worse. Many of the vendors had packed up their wares and disappeared into the mist.

As she turned down an alley, Lucy found herself on a street lined with dingy-looking houses in need of paint and shacks surrounded by rubble. The broken windows were stuffed with newspaper and rags and piles of night soil and horse manure were heaped beside doorsteps.

From a gin palace came the loud shouts of men and the wild shrieks of a woman's laughter. Lucy wrinkled her nose, for the air smelled of dog dung, smoke, and vinegar from the pickle factory at the end of the street. She trembled to think that Glory was lost and alone in this ugly, frightening world.

In desperation, Lucy turned and headed back down the street. But when she reached Nuggins Rag and Bone Shop, she found the window dark and the door locked tight. There was no sign of Glory anywhere.

Lucy sank down on the Nuggins's doorstep, beside herself with worry, not knowing where to turn. But when a constable approached she had to leave fast.

Her fear of being sent back to the workhouse was now greater than ever, for if she were to be sent back alone, she would never find Glory.

Lucy dashed across the street and was almost run down by a horse pulling a trap. It wasn't until she turned a bend that she slowed her pace and finally came to a stop and rested against a lamppost. Her heart raced as she tried to catch her breath. Her feet ached and her fingers were numb with the cold.

How cold was Glory? How frightened must the little one be? Was she in danger? Or was she hiding, somewhere safe from harm, waiting for her big sister to find her?

But what safe harbor is there in this dark and dangerous city, Lucy wondered, that could shelter an orphan girl from the clutches of scoundrels and police alike? Where could such a place be? As exhausted as she was, a voice inside kept her going.

"Keep moving," it said. "Keep looking."

Wiping her runny nose on the cuff of her sleeve, Lucy started back into the wind. She took a deep breath and felt a pang of sorrow, for the intoxicating aroma of fried sausage was suddenly on the breeze. As Lucy stood breathing in the delicious scent that drifted from an opened door, she couldn't help but to think of the wonderful meal she had planned to share with Glory.

She reached into her pocket then, to feel for the penny, to wrap her fingers around the one piece of good luck they had had. But when she did, Lucy was horrified at what she found. The penny was gone! With a cry, she poked her finger right through the threadbare material and realized that the coin had fallen through the hole.

Suddenly, the overwhelming loss of so much was more than she could bear. Lucy found herself stumbling down the footpath in a daze of disbelief. She had lost the only money they'd ever had. She had traded away the only thing that Glory had ever wished for. But worst of all was the thought that she might never see her little sister again.

Lucy's regret was so sharp, her exhaustion so great, her sorrow so deep, she collapsed on the stoop of a nearby shop. It was then that she heard a familiar voice call.

"If it ain't the ninny from the country!"

CHAPTER SIXTEEN

UCY LOOKED UP TO SEE THE BOY IN THE tattered coat and paper hat before her. In his arms was a small child with a head of tangled blonde curls.

"Glory!" Lucy cried, pulling her sister from him. "Oh, Glory, you gave me such a fright!"

"You shouldn't 'ave left me all alone in that shop like you did, Luce," Glory sobbed.

"I'm sorry," Lucy said, wiping the tears from her sister's cheeks. Then she turned to the boy. "I'm ever so grateful . . ."

"Nick," Glory finished her sentence. "His name is Nick. He helped me find you."

"Nick Button, at your service." The boy grinned as he tipped his paper hat.

"Thank you kindly, Nick Button," Lucy said. "I don't know how to repay you. . . ." She reached into her pocket and pulled out the piece of scone she had saved from the doll shop.

"'Tweren't nothing." Nick shrugged. "Wasn't expecting no payment, though I'm happy to accept," he said, reaching for the scone and quickly shoving it into his mouth. "I jest can't stand to see anyone cry," he admitted through a mouthful. "'Specially little girls."

Lucy turned to look at him closer. He appeared to be about nine or ten years old. And though his face was smudged with soot and covered with scratches, Lucy saw kindness in Nick Button's dark eyes. His sympathy seemed so genuine that Lucy quickly forgave him for calling her a ninny.

"Now that I get a better look at you both, I can see you ain't from the country at all," Nick commented. "Come from the workhouse, 'ave you then?"

Lucy's shoulders stiffened and her smile instantly disappeared. "How do you know?" she whispered.

"I heard all about it from your sister here." Nick shrugged. "Besides, I know lots of people who spent time in those awful places. But don't worry," he added. "Your secret is good with me."

Lucy relaxed, then proceeded to tell him how she and Glory had come to be on their own in the city. It felt so good to be sharing all that was troubling her that she couldn't stop herself. In a rush of words she poured out her heart, telling everything. But when she got to the part about how she and Glory had escaped from Grimstone, she stopped abruptly, fearing she had revealed too much.

"You won't tell anyone?" she whispered anxiously.

"Don't worry, no Constable is a friend to me," Nick assured her. "And, in truth, he'd sooner see me locked up than look at me. Of course, he'd 'ave to catch me first," he added with a grin.

"I happens to know some boys wot lit out of that house," he continued. "My friend Jim Binney is one. Ain't no shame in that. Takes a good lot of cheek and cunning to break out. Never heard of a girl who'd done it, though."

He looked at Lucy with such admiration, she felt herself blush.

"Lucy," Glory suddenly interrupted. "Where is Morning Glory?"

Lucy hesitated. "We've got no money and no food," she finally replied. "The scissors were gone. We had nothing left to sell."

Glory let out a gasp and brought her hand to her mouth. The little one blinked hard as her lower lip trembled. "Do you mean . . ."

Lucy nodded slowly. "Sold her, yes, I did," Lucy said, lowering her eyes. "For a penny."

She went on to explain about her job at the doll shop and the coin Miss Thimblebee paid her and how she'd lost it.

"Never trust a penny to a pocket, is what I always say," Nick piped up. "All me money goes directly in me shoes. 'Tis the safest place. Of course, all I've got is me toes in there now . . ."

"But Luce," Glory cried, her face flushed and her eyes filling with tears. "You said she'd be mine! You said one day I'd find her and when I did I should be able to keep her with me forever and ever! 'Tis what you always said at the end of the story!"

"Oh," Lucy exclaimed. "It was wickedly cruel of me to ever promise such things. I know that now." She burned with shame at having told such stories about the doll to Glory. "You see, Glory, 'tisn't easy being a big sister. You can make big mistakes. And now that we've no one to look after us, I've got to do whatever I must to keep us alive. 'Twas the only reason I thought to sell Morning Glory in the first place. Don't you see?"

As the tears streamed down her cheeks, Glory's head of dirty curls bobbed up and down, and her frail little body shook with a sob she would not let out. She offered no words of resistance, as Lucy knew she wouldn't, for heartbreak was part and parcel of the life they'd known.

But as Lucy watched the little one's dirty fingers twisting the frayed ends of her shawl, she felt her own eyes fill with tears. For she feared this latest wound cut deeper than most. Lucy knew that Morning Glory meant much more than idle play to a child such as Glory. To an orphaned girl growing up in the grim shadows of the workhouse, a doll to call her own offered the hope of a brighter, happier life. And Lucy suddenly worried that it was this small glimmer of hope that kept her sister alive. Without it to cling to she feared her sister might slip away as easily as little Aggie Crofter and the others.

Meanwhile, the usually boisterous Nick Button had been standing silently by. But silence was not something Nick was especially good at. And the sight of two girls weeping was something he simply could not abide.

"Here now," he said, clearing his throat. "I've an idea. 'Tis a very big city this, and like you, I've no one to turn to, no family to speak of. Hooked up with a couple of moonlight flitters . . ."

"Moonlight flitters?" Lucy repeated.

"You know, them wot can't pay their rent, so they flit out in the middle of the night so as not to get caught. We had to part company so we wouldn't be recognized. Now I'm back on me own and ain't having much luck. Maybe if we three teamed up, we'd all have a warm place to sleep and a bit of food to eat."

"But how?" Lucy asked with a look of surprise.

"I could look after Glory during the day, while you

work in the doll shop," Nick explained. "Then come nightfall, after closing, you unlock the shop and let us both in."

"Both?" Lucy repeated, anxiously.

Nick nodded. "You see, I'm a bit down on me luck of late. Been tumbling to make some pennies in front of the old Opera House doing headstands, back flips, and the like. But on account of the bad weather, people aren't as likely to stand around to watch. After I do me tumbles, there's no one to pass the hat to and so I had to sell it."

"Sell it?"

"Me hat, that is." Nick sighed. " 'Tis how I come by wearing this paper cap. I've only me shoes left to sell and I'd sorely hate to see them go."

Lucy looked down to see that below his short, tattered trousers he had on two very different shoes. One was black leather and pointed, with a proper buckle, while the other was a big, brown floppy thing, tied with twine. He had a thin, tattered sock on his left foot, while his right remained bare and his bony little ankle was chafed and cherry red from the cold.

"How'd you like to go tumbling with me, Glory?" Nick asked.

But Lucy answered before Glory could. " 'Tis awfully cold for her to be out in the weather all day. She's been coughing and shouldn't catch a chill."

"Oh, a cough can come in right handy. Could bring in an extra ha'penny or two out of sympathy," Nick said thoughtfully. But seeing Lucy's frown, he quickly amended this statement. "Of course, there's no need for her to get chilled. The other lads and I only tumble for a short while, afore and after the shows. If we need to get warm, we can always stop by the oyster stall beside the King's Mug public house. The oysterman always keeps a good fire going to warm his hands and if we run errands for him, he'll let us sit by the fire. Or there's Bob the Rat Catcher. He might have some work for me."

"Catching rats?" Lucy asked.

"Aye, there's many a fine house wot's overrun with 'em. Glory can come along while I catch. I know a few of the cooks in the big houses, and they sometimes gives me a crust and lets me sit by the fire in the kitchen after I've caught me a bagful. For you see, the cooks hate rats wot nest in their cupboards and eat up their vittles."

"I shouldn't fancy catching rats," Glory murmured.

"Don't you worry none, Glory Mop," Nick told her. "You can wait inside where it's warm while I hunt. And if I can catch a bagful, why, cook will be so happy she'll probably treat us to an apple or maybe even an orange!"

Glory's eyes brightened at the prospect of fruit.

Lucy could see that her sister had taken a liking to
Nick Button. Lucy liked him as well, though she worried about breaking her promise to Miss Thimblebee.
But if she didn't have someone to look after Glory
during the day, she wouldn't be able to work in the
doll shop at all.

"So wot do you think?" Nick grinned. "We can all
help each other. You haven't anyone else to turn to,
'ave you?" He held out a grimy hand to her.

Lucy didn't have to think his offer over for long.
As she listened to the wheeze in Glory's chest, she
thought of the girl Florrie Nuggins had told them
about, the girl who had been found frozen to death
on the street. Then she thought about the warm
stove at Thimblebee's shop.

"No," Lucy said. "We've no one."

And as she reached out to shake Nick Button's
hand, Lucy Wolcott felt as if a heavy weight had
been lifted from her shoulders. She and Glory had
found a friend. And with his help, she could take the
job at the doll shop, a job that could give them food
and a warm place to sleep. Lucy hoped with all her
heart that their luck would hold and that together
they could somehow manage to stay alive.

CHAPTER SEVENTEEN

HEN LUCY FINALLY REACHED NUMBER NINE Mulberry Lane, she looked back at Glory and Nick walking in the opposite direction to the oyster stall by the King's Mug. Nick promised to bring Glory to the doll shop later that night. And Lucy promised Glory that if she was good and didn't leave Nick's side, she would be able to see Morning Glory again.

Lucy watched anxiously as the two disappeared around a corner. Then she looked up at the darkening sky and whispered a prayer.

"Please, Lord," she prayed. "Watch over my sister and keep her safe."

Quickly she climbed the brick steps and with a nervous hand, turned the brass knob on the shop's door.

Once inside, Lucy found Miss Thimblebee behind the counter, counting up the notes and coins in her register box. Bess and the others were tying on their bonnets and reaching for their shawls. One by one they took their leave.

As she waited, Lucy could not ignore the fanciful allure of the doll shop's display room. In the glow of the lamplight, a twinkling magic seemed to take hold. Once again she felt as if she'd stepped into another world, a dreamworld where only the beauty of white lace and the sweetness of a doll's smile were allowed. And so many smiles there were.

"Ah, Miss Wolcott, here you are at last," Miss Thimblebee clucked, looking over the top of her spectacles. "Of course, if you're to work in the window, those raggedy old gray skirts shall never do. You must have a proper frock. We'll see about that tomorrow. For now you may come with me."

Lucy followed her through the paisley curtain back to the workroom, where she found a plate and a cup of tea had been set out on a little table before a glowing stove. On the plate was a portion of suet pudding, a potato, and a biscuit.

'Tis a feast! Lucy thought, her mouth watering at the sight of such a generous meal.

"You'll find your supper here, and the kettle is on the trivet if you need more tea. I don't like my dolls shivering at night," Miss Thimblebee added, reaching for a scuttle of coal from a bucket beside the stove. "So be sure to stoke the fire well, before you fall asleep."

Lucy watched as she opened the stove's door and added the coal.

"The shop is to stay warm and cozy," Miss Thimblebee said with a smile.

Lucy stared in awe. The warmth from the stove was warm beyond her wildest dreams.

"The candles are here in the drawer with snuffer and matches," Miss Thimblebee went on to explain. "Be sure to keep the drawer closed, or the mice will make a meal of the tallow. There are blankets in the bottom drawer of the cupboard and the water closet is just there." She pointed to a narrow door at the back of the room.

Her voice took on a more serious tone as she laid a wrinkled hand on Lucy's shoulder. "My dolls mean a great deal to me, my dear, and I am entrusting their care to you. Now, some would think me foolish to pick a girl such as yourself, come off the street as you have, with no references to speak of."

She looked into Lucy eyes and smiled warmly. "But truth be known, I have a very good feeling about you, Lucy Wolcott, for as I always say, a good heart is hard to hide."

Lucy nervously lowered her eyes to the floor. All her life she'd been battered by the bitter winds of hardship. Now she stood frozen in silence as the old woman's kindness wrapped around her like a warm quilt. She didn't want to breathe, for fear it would all disappear.

"Go on, then," Miss Thimblebee urged. "Don't let me keep you from your supper. I've a few last-minute things to attend to before we close up." She turned and quickly disappeared through the curtain.

Lucy walked to the table and leaned over to smell the pudding. The scent was so delicious she almost fainted with hunger. She quickly devoured a small part of it and some of the potato and biscuit as well, leaving the rest on the plate to save for Nick and Glory.

As she sipped her tea by the warm stove, Lucy couldn't stop thinking of the two and wondering how they were doing.

But her worries were suddenly interrupted by the sound of a voice. Lucy turned to look at the paisley curtain, for she could hear someone whispering in the display room.

Who could Miss Thimblebee be talking to this late in the day? she wondered. The doll-makers had all gone and the last customer had left ages ago.

As quietly as she could, Lucy peeked through the curtain. There in the lamplight, she spied the old woman chattering away to a beautiful dark-haired doll that stood on the counter.

"Oh, Charlotte," Miss Thimblebee murmured, reaching for the doll's porcelain hand. "So many Christmases have come and gone since first we opened our doors. Another Christmas is upon us, and my heart still breaks, my heart still breaks."

Lucy thought it most curious to see the old woman talking to the doll as if it were a real person. And she noticed that Miss Thimblebee's voice had become softer and full of emotion. But as Lucy listened at the curtain, she felt a tug at her own heart, for the old woman's whispered conversation with the doll reminded Lucy of her many whispered talks with Glory back at Grimstone. She pulled the curtain back a bit so that she could hear more, when Miss Thimblebee suddenly caught sight of her.

"Oh, my stars!" Mrs. Thimblebee cried out, her face flushed with embarrassment. "I didn't see you there. Gave me quite a start, you did! Do you need something, my dear?"

"Oh, no, no," Lucy stammered. "I'm so sorry. I thought I heard something. . . ."

"Perhaps you heard the night watchman call the hour," Miss Thimblebee said, her voice growing chilly and her manner stiff. "Yes, I heard him myself, and 'tis well past the time when we should be fussing about here, I daresay. We've a busy day ahead of us tomorrow and you shall need your rest."

Without another word, she turned and picked up the doll from the counter and gently placed her in a glass case that hung on the wall. Lucy watched as she reached for a small brass key that hung from a silver chain at her waist.

"Sweet dreams, Charlotte," Miss Thimblebee whispered as she fitted the key into the case's lock. Then she reached for her bonnet and cape that hung on a hook beside the door.

"I'll be going now," Miss Thimblebee said, turning to look back at Lucy. "I'm just down the street at Number Fourteen. You're to fetch me if any foul play arises, but save for that or fire, you're not to open the door for anyone."

She lowered her voice to a cautious whisper as she lit a candle and handed it to Lucy. "These are dangerous times we live in," she said, turning down the big brass lamp that hung over the counter. "One can't be too careful, what with all the scoundrels and tosspots lurking about. Once I lock the door, you're not to open it to anyone. Not a soul is to enter afore I return in the morning, is that understood?"

"Yes, mum," Lucy whispered, casting her eyes downward. She longed to tell her about Glory and their situation, but her fear of being sent back to Grimstone was so great, she dared not say a word.

"Good night, my dear," Miss Thimblebee called.

There was a jangle of bells as the door slammed shut, followed by the sound of a key turning in the lock and a loud click.

Alone at last, Lucy hurried to the display window and looked out, hoping to catch a glimpse of Nick and Glory. In the glow of the street lamp she could see a "tater man" pushing a wheelbarrow half full of potatoes up the street.

Behind him came a "lavender lady," with her basket on her arm and a baby in a sling. The woman's face was drawn and tired from a day's selling out on the cold street. Her thin shawl blew back around her in the wind.

How cold was Glory? Was Nick looking after her? Lucy wished that they would come now, but it still wasn't safe.

She hoped Nick was waiting for the streets to empty and the shop windows to darken. But what if he didn't wait? What if he came now and he and Glory were seen?

To still her racing mind, Lucy checked the fire, then walked through the display room, gazing at the many smiling faces in the candlelight. She stopped to look at the fancily dressed lady dolls in lace and satin. As she moved from one doll to the next, Lucy imagined which one she would choose if she were a well-born girl and had the money to buy a doll of her own. Finally, she stopped at a glass case that hung behind the counter. There Miss Thimblebee's lovely Charlotte stood.

Lifting her candle, Lucy stared at the smiling dark-haired doll. She was clearly the most beautiful doll in the shop. Lucy wondered why Miss Thimblebee kept her locked away in a case. And as her eye traveled over the doll's sweet face and apricot gown, Lucy remembered Miss Thimblebee's words, "My heart still breaks, my heart still breaks . . ."

A lump rose in Lucy's throat as she thought of another doll, a doll she suddenly longed to see. With candle in hand she searched the shelves behind the counter. Having no luck there, she made her way back through the paisley curtains to the workroom.

Passing her candle over the many wooden shelves, Lucy discovered bags of stuffing, cushions full of pins, and jars of bright paint. She hunted through baskets of arms and boxes of legs. She pushed aside heads without hair and faces without smiles. She looked behind jars full of buttons and spools of colored threads. But nowhere could she find what she was looking for.

Finally, Lucy spied a little heap of mud-stained rags lying in a box at the far corner of the shelf.

"Morning Glory!" Lucy cried, pulling the filthy

old doll from the box and hugging her tight. "Oh, Morning Glory, if only I hadn't had to sell you!"

With the old doll cradled in her arms, Lucy huddled next to the fire to wait for Nick and Glory. She said one last prayer for their safety before her eyes grew heavy and she fell into a deep sleep.

Later that night, long after most gentlefolk had taken to their beds, a reddened hand reached up to Thimblebee's plum-colored door. Lucy awoke to a *rap-rap-rap* on the door's glass pane. Her heart raced at the sound of it. They were here at last! They were safe!

With a candle in one hand and Morning Glory in another, Lucy hurried through the darkness of the display room to unbolt the door. But as she held up her light in the opened doorway, she suddenly let out a cry so sharp it pierced the night air and stirred the blackbirds that roosted on Thimblebee's roof. For instead of Nick and Glory, one large blue suit with a gruff voice and a bushy black mustache stood waiting at the door!

"Begging your pardon, didn't mean to startle you, miss," the Constable grumbled. "But seems we've got some trouble brewing tonight."

Chapter Eighteen

UCY BARELY FELT THE HOT WAX THAT DRIPPED down onto her trembling hand as she tried to speak.

"Tr . . . trouble?" she managed to sputter.

"Aye." The Constable sighed. "There's been a burglary just a few doors up, at Sampson's Bake Shop. A thief made off with almost twenty pounds and all of the baker's cherry tarts to boot! We're alerting all the shops and houses on this street. Check your doors and windows, Miss. Make sure they're locked fast, for the thief is still on the loose. If you hear anything suspicious or see any strange characters skulking about you're to report it to us at once."

"Yes, sir," Lucy said, trying to steady her voice. "Just as you say, sir."

"Right, then, I'll be on me way," the Constable replied. Lucy began to close the door when his large hand reached out to hold it open.

"Hang on," he said. "I don't remember seeing you on this street before."

Lucy's face went white. "M-miss Thimblebee, sh-she . . . just hired me," she stammered. "I'm to be her new Hearts Girl."

"Aye," the Constable said with a nod. "Well, Miss Hearts Girl, I warrant you'll be seeing the likes of me again right soon."

"Sir?" Lucy squeaked. She was sure that he meant he was coming back to arrest her and take her back to Grimstone.

"To do a bit of Christmas shopping meself," the Constable said with a wink. "For I've a little girl of me own. And I've promised her a doll. So keep them locked up safe, now, Miss Hearts Girl." He tapped his hat with his stick and turned to leave.

Lucy closed the door, then fell back against it, partly from relief, but partly from worry. Nick and Glory should have arrived at the shop hours ago. But now, with the Constable on the lookout for the thief, how would they slip by unnoticed? What if the Constable found them and sent Glory back to the workhouse? And what of the thief? What if Nick and Glory ran into him in the dark? What if Nick was the thief? The thought was too terrible. Lucy sank to the floor with the old doll still in her arms and soon fell into a fitful sleep.

It was sometime later that Lucy was awakened by another *rap-rap-rap* at the pane behind her.

"Who's there?" She trembled in the dark.

"Open up, Luce," a little voice answered from behind the closed door. "'Tis awfully cold out here!"

Lucy unbolted the door, and didn't hide her joy at seeing Nick and Glory standing before her, shivering in their threadbare rags. Their eyes were watery and their noses were red from walking in the wind and cold.

"Oh, thank heavens! You've come at last!" Lucy whispered, holding her light up to guide them inside to the fire.

"Ah." Glory sighed. "'Tis ever so warm in here!"

"Thought me foot was going to freeze, certain sure," Nick grumbled as he reached down to rub his bare ankle. "We'd of been here sooner but for the Constable going up and down and waking up the whole street."

"Luce! You kept your promise!" Glory cried out on seeing the old doll in her sister's arms.

"And she's yours to hold all night long if you like," Lucy said, handing her the doll.

Glory's smiling little face shone in the candlelight as she hugged the doll to her.

"Why, 'tis lucky you didn't freeze to death out in that cold," Lucy said as she rubbed Glory's chapped cheeks with her hands.

"Speaking of luck," Nick said, reaching into his

pocket. "We had the good fortune to spend most of the day inside, hunting rats."

"A cook gave us a biscuit each," Glory said excitedly.

"And if that weren't lucky enough, on the way here we found all sorts of good things by a greengrocer's cart." Lucy watched as he pulled some limp cabbage leaves from his pocket. "And look at this fine specimen here!" He held up a small onion. "Now if we had us some water we could make a broth."

"There's a kettle I can put on the stove in the back room," Lucy told him. "And I've got some potato we can add to it."

She held up her candle and began to guide them through the display room when Glory stopped short.

"Oh, Luce," the little one gasped, looking at the many smiling faces of the dolls in the candlelight. "The dolls! They're so beautiful!"

"Yes, they are," Lucy replied. "And look at these here, why, they look like princesses, with crowns upon their heads and jewels in their hair!"

"If my Morning Glory had a crown, she'd look like a princess, too," Glory declared. Taking Glory's hand Lucy guided her through the paisley curtains to the back room. Nick found the kettle and began to add the onions and cabbage leaves.

A cheerful mood came over the three as they sat before the warmth of the stove. Lucy crumbled what was left of the potato into the kettle, and she laid out the biscuit and pudding she had saved. Glory began to cough and Lucy put a cup of warm tea in her hands and set her next to the fire. When she wrapped the thick quilt Miss Thimblebee had given her around Glory, the little one cried out with pleasure.

"Oh, Luce!" she sighed. "It's so lovely here with the fire and the tea and a warm blanket. 'Tis just like you said it was at home with Mother and Father when we were a family."

Lucy felt a warm glow inside and out as she added another shovelful of coal to the fire. *If only we could stay here forever,* she thought.

Nick told funny stories and they had themselves a merry feast. For all their difficulties, there was much to celebrate. Lucy had Glory back, Nick Button had a place to warm his feet, and Glory had Morning Glory in her arms.

Later that night, as Nick curled up on one side of the stove to sleep and Lucy and Glory snuggled together on the cot Miss Thimblebee had set up, Glory was still whispering to the old doll.

"I shall love you forever and ever, Morning Glory," Lucy heard her say.

"You understand, she's not yours to keep," Lucy said sleepily. "Morning Glory belongs to Thimblebee's now."

"Yes, I know," Glory murmured. "But even if I won't always be able to hold her in my arms, I can still hold my love for her here in my heart, forever and ever. Isn't that so, Luce?"

As the blackbirds on Thimblebee's roof silently folded their wings under a winter's moon, and the passing hour brought them one day closer to Christmas, Lucy Wolcott smiled and whispered, "Yes."

But it was a sad smile, for she knew that the job of Hearts Girl would not last forever, and come the day after Christmas, they would all be out in the cold once again.

Chapter Nineteen

HE NEXT MORNING, THE THREE AWOKE before the lamplighter had made his rounds. Living as long as they had in the workhouse, the Wolcott sisters were accustomed to rising before the sun. It was only after many promises from Nick to keep a close eye on Glory that Lucy let go of her sister and allowed her to leave. Standing at the doll-shop door, Lucy anxiously watched Glory slip her little hand into Nick's. And as the two disappeared into the darkness, Lucy said a quick prayer.

"I am trusting her care to you, Lord," she whispered. "You and Nick Button. I pray I've done right. And that you'll see them back safely tonight."

Once they were gone, Lucy hurried to put more coal on the fire and to wash out the kettle and return Morning Glory to her box on the shelf. She was careful not to leave any trace of her visitors behind. When Lucy was through, she lay down before the fire to rest. It was sometime later that she heard the ringing of bells at the front door and Miss Thimblebee's voice directing the charwoman to be sure to wipe down the shelves. "It won't do to have dust balls on my dolls," she said.

As the doll-makers arrived there was a good deal of hustle and bustle all through the shop. The excitement of the holiday was in the air. Bess hung a wreath on the door, while Emma and Iris decorated the window with paper stars and holly.

Because she was to work in the window, Lucy's appearance was given special attention. Miss Thimblebee insisted she have a bath. Bess and Iris filled a tub in the back room with water and lit a fire next to it. Lucy cringed at the sight of the tub. For twice a year all the children at Grimstone were made to take baths. And twice a year they gritted their teeth so they might endure the torture of the water, which was either scalding hot or icy cold.

But much to her surprise Lucy found the water warm and soothing. Iris handed her a sweet-smelling ball of soap. After she was washed and dried from head to toe, and wrapped in yards of clean, warm flannel, Miss Thimblebee turned her attention to Lucy's hair.

She ran a brush through Lucy's wet chestnut curls. The old woman was so gentle and so loving in her touch, Lucy felt a shivery tingle with each stroke.

"You have such beautiful, thick hair, my girl," Miss

Thimblebee murmured. "Why, looking at you now so clean and pretty, you look very much like my Charlotte did."

Lucy closed her eyes then, and found herself imagining it was her own mother speaking so softly in her ear. Finally, when Miss Thimblebee was through, she tied a black silk bow in Lucy's hair. Next Lucy was helped into a clean blue dress and crisp white pinafore.

Everyone oohed and ahhed over Lucy's transformation, but it was Miss Thimblebee herself who seemed most pleased of all.

"Truly a Thimblebee's Hearts Girl, if ever I saw one," the old woman said, clapping her hands.

Lucy blushed as she looked down at the clean, white folds of her pinafore. She could hardly believe her eyes, for she could not remember ever having worn a garment so white or so new. But even more astonishing to her was the discovery of the pinafore's small pocket edged in lace.

Lucy blinked in amazement, for though it was no more than a few inches long, the little frill of white lace seemed as luxurious to her as the Queen's own finery.

"Bless my soul, I'm wearing lace!" Lucy whispered under her breath. She could hardly contain her surprise and delight, and kept stealing looks down at the pocket to be sure the lace was still there.

"'Tis lucky you're just about the same size as Mary," Emma said as she smoothed down Lucy's collar. "Though when she comes back after Christmas I daresay we'll have to let the hem out again. For as me mother always says, after a sickness most children gain in inches what they lose in weight."

With a pang of sorrow, Lucy's bright smile suddenly faded at the mention of Mary. For it was Mary's job, not hers. And it was Mary's fine dress she was wearing. Come the day after Christmas Mary would return to Thimblebee's Doll Shop and take it all away from Lucy.

"And now her thimble," Miss Thimblebee said. Lucy watched as the old woman reached for a wooden box on the workroom shelf. When she lifted the lid, Lucy gasped at the sight of a small silver thimble sitting on a bed of blue velvet.

"'Tis the only silver thimble in the shop," Emma whispered excitedly.

"And 'tis only the Hearts Girl who may wear it," Iris added.

"'Twould fit no other," Bess said with a shake of her head.

"Go on, child, try it on," commanded Miss Thimblebee.

With a trembling hand Lucy reached for the thimble and nervously placed it on her middle finger.

"A perfect fit!" Miss Thimblebee beamed. "Now let the workday begin."

In the glow of the early morning lamplight, fingers slipped into thimbles, floss was threaded through needles, and brushes dipped into paint. Bolts of satin were unrolled, sacks of flock were split open, patterns were laid, chalk dust flew, and everyone was soon lost in the magic of making dolls.

It seemed Lucy truly did possess a natural talent for giving hearts. With a knowing eye she studied each doll placed before her that day. Whether a modeled wax portrait doll in a gold brocade cloak, or a fine porcelain beauty in a sheer dimity gown, Lucy seemed to know the heart each deserved. Without aid of chalk or pencil, with neither patterns nor pins, she was able to fashion a heart so true to each doll that they left her hands with the glow of completion. For there is nothing so unfinished, so incomplete, as a doll without a heart.

Working at a little table in the display window, Lucy looked up often to see the many Christmas shoppers hurrying past. From their arms hung baskets full of parcels and boxes tied with bright ribbons.

Never having had a Christmas present in all the years she'd lived at Grimstone, Lucy watched with utmost interest now, wondering just what sorts of things were in those baskets and boxes tied with bows.

Later that day, Bess called Lucy from the window to join the others for tea and crumpets in the work-room. While Miss Thimblebee poured, Emma passed the sugar bowl and Iris passed the cream. As the doll-makers sat quietly discussing the merits of silk over satin for a new doll's gown, Lucy sat in silence. The experience of "tea" with such things as china cups, teaspoons, lumps of sugar, and fresh cream had left her quite speechless.

When no one was looking, she slipped an extra crumpet into her pocket. At the sound of the front doorbells ringing, Miss Thimblebee rose to her feet and teatime came to an end.

"Mustn't keep the customer waiting," Miss Thimble-bee said cheerily. "Oh, and Iris," she called over her shoulder, "be sure to finish that sprig of silk holly for Charlotte's bonnet."

"Yes, mum," Iris replied.

"'Tis a wonder how she fusses over that Charlotte," Emma whispered once Miss Thimblebee was gone. It was then that Lucy recalled the old woman whisper-ing to the doll the night before.

"Yes," Bess agreed, taking her place back at the worktable. "I can't imagine what she should do if any-thing were to happen to that doll."

"But what if someone were to buy Charlotte?" Lucy asked.

"Bite your tongue!" Emma gasped. "Miss Thimble-bee would never part with her."

"'Tis why she has that NOT FOR SALE sign over her case," added Iris.

"Charlotte is very special to Miss Thimblebee," Bess said.

"She is quite lovely," Lucy agreed. "But there are lots of other lovely dolls in the shop. What is it that makes her so special?"

Bess looked over to the closed curtain and lowered her voice to a whisper. "Charlotte was made long ago by Miss Thimblebee's sister."

"Her sister?" Lucy asked.

"Yes. You see, when Miss Thimblebee first opened this shop, she was a young woman and her only sister, Charlotte, was just a girl. The Thimblebee girls were orphaned quite young. It was Charlotte who first gave the dolls their hearts. She had a talent for it, I daresay, much like your own." She smiled.

"Where is Charlotte now?" Lucy asked.

Bess's smile faded. "'Twas a sad business, that. For one winter, close to Christmas, Charlotte took sick with consumption and died. It was a terrible blow to Miss Thimblebee. Surely it was. She loved her little sister so."

Lucy thought of her own sister out in the cold, with her cough and threadbare clothes. She felt a painful tug at her heart.

Poor Miss Thimblebee, Lucy thought. *How does one bear such sadness?*

"And so Miss Thimblebee named the doll for her sister," Emma continued.

"Yes," Bess said, nodding. "For she was the last doll to receive a heart from Charlotte Thimblebee's hand. Why, that doll has stood in her glass case these three and thirty years now. I daresay she means more to Miss Thimblebee than all the dolls in this shop."

Later, as Lucy sat and sewed in the window, her thoughts turned to two very different dolls and the hearts that held them close. She thought of Morning Glory and how much her sister had grown to love her. And she thought of Charlotte, the doll Miss Thimblebee found so dear.

With each heart she made now, Lucy added an extra stitch to secure it in place. For she was beginning to understand just how fragile a thing a heart could be.

Chapter Twenty

ATER THAT NIGHT, LONG AFTER ALL THE doll-makers had gone home and the shop windows along the street had darkened, Lucy once again took up her needle and thread. But it was not a heart she was sewing. It was a small patchwork dress, pieced together from the scraps she had found on the floor. Sitting beside the warm stove in Thimblebee's back room, her fingers hurried to finish.

Just as she had taken her last stitch and tied her last knot, there came a knocking at the plum-colored door. Once again she let out a sigh of relief at the welcome sound.

"Oh, Luce!" Glory gasped as she walked in the door. "Look at you! Why, you look like a princess!"

"'Tis the same old me," Lucy laughed as she twirled around and around. "I've been given a bath — and a new dress."

"To keep?" Glory cried.

"Just to work in," Lucy explained.

"You look like a doll yourself," Nick marveled. "Even your hair shines!"

Lucy proudly shook her head of shiny chestnut curls. Glory began to clap her dirty hands, but stopped suddenly at the start of another long cough.

"'Twas bitter cold out there today," Nick told Lucy as she helped Glory to the back-room stove.

Lucy felt a pang of guilt that she had spent such a happy, comfortable day, while her sister had had to suffer in the miserable cold.

"Even with Glory helping, we only brought in enough to buy but one mug of cider all day," Nick added.

"Glory helping?" Lucy asked.

"I hold the hat while Nick tumbles," Glory said weakly.

"And she did a right good job of it, too," Nick added.

"But I thought you said you'd keep her warm. Why, she's half frozen," Lucy cried, as she wrapped Glory in a quilt.

"I tried to find work with Bob the Rat Catcher, but he had gone for the day," Nick explained. "There was nothing left to do but try our luck tumbling. When that didn't bring in more than a ha'penny we tried begging on Pettycoat Lane. We didn't do much better there, but at least we got to warm our hands by the chestnut carts and the oyster stalls. And on account of the holiday season, we did come by these."

Lucy watched as he emptied his pockets onto the wooden table, pulling out a handful of nuts and a dried piece of cod.

"'Tis almost Christmas." Nick grinned. "The very best season of the year. For cooks and costers tend to be more generous with the gifts they hand out. Such as this 'ere." He pulled out a dark-spotted turnip from his pocket and held it up. "Did you ever see such a beauty as this one? 'Tis only a little bit rotten. A coster wot sells vegetables to the better sorts give it to me. One of the greater gifts of the day."

"Have you ever had the kind of gift that comes wrapped in a box, Nick?" Lucy suddenly asked. "One that is tied with a bow?"

"Well, no," Nick answered, as he bit into a rotten part of the turnip and spit it out. "I can't say as I have. The gifts wot come my way are usually of the over-ripe variety, you see. Wot's gone a little bad and the cook's about to toss out or a coster's wanting to throw away."

"If you could have that other kind of Christmas gift that came in a box and was tied in a bow, what should it be?" Lucy asked.

Nick cocked his head. "Could it be anything at all?"

Lucy nodded. "Anything you fancy."

"Then 'tis easy," Nick answered, pointing down to his shoe. "I'd have me a sock for me other foot. One knit of the thickest wool. Then I wouldn't have to be changing the only one I got from one foot to the other to keep me toes from freezing."

Lucy looked over to Glory. "I don't suppose you need to tell us what you'd fancy." She went over to the shelf and took Morning Glory down, placing her in her little sister's waiting arms. Then she presented her with the patchwork dress she had made.

"Oh, Luce! It's beautiful!" Glory cried as she slipped it over Morning Glory's head. The old doll seemed to be smiling proudly in her colorful dress of blue satin patches, yellow silk, and pink taffeta squares.

"She looks as beautiful as any doll here," Glory proclaimed.

Nick looked over at Glory and shook his head. "You mean to tell me that if you could have any doll in this 'ere shop, you'd still fancy that old thing?"

Glory nodded.

"Even if you could have one of those lovely dolls in the velvet gowns?" Lucy asked. "Or the one up in the case?"

"Which one is that?" Glory asked.

So Lucy took the candle and with Glory and Nick following close behind, she guided them into the display room. Once they got to the counter, Lucy stopped and held the candle up so that it shone on Charlotte's smiling face.

A hush fell over Glory and her eyes shone brightly.

"Oh, Luce," she finally whispered. "Her face is so very beautiful! And she has such fine silky curls. I never knew a doll could be so lovely!"

"She's the loveliest doll in the shop," Lucy added.

"But there's something about her," Glory said, hugging Morning Glory close. "She must be dreadfully lonely, sitting all alone in that case."

It was then that Lucy told them the unhappy story of Miss Thimblebee's little sister, Charlotte, and how the doll came to be locked away behind glass.

On hearing this, Glory cried so uncontrollably that Lucy had to console her for a long while. For Glory, having known the heartache of loss while still in her baby's cradle, felt the deepest sympathy for anyone who suffered.

Later Lucy watched as Glory sat before the fire with Morning Glory in her arms. Lucy could see that the sweet weariness of Glory's little face seemed to match the weariness of the weathered old doll. Lucy was certain that the only doll Glory could ever want was there in her arms.

"And how about you, Lucy?" Nick suddenly asked.

"You never did tell us wot Christmas gift you should fancy."

Lucy thought. "If I could have anything at all," she finally said, "I should fancy a plum pudding."

"Like Mother's?" Glory asked.

"Yes," Lucy smiled. "Just like Mother's."

"Did you really have a mother once, to make you a Christmas pudding?" Nick asked.

"Oh, yes," Glory told him. "Lucy remembers. She tells all about it in the Christmas story." Glory turned to Lucy then. "Go on, Luce," she pleaded. "Do tell it so Nick can hear."

And so it was that as the winter's wind whistled over the cobblestones on Mulberry Lane and Nick Button's turnip simmered in the kettle on the stove, Lucy Wolcott's whispered words filled the doll shop's back room.

"'Twas almost Christmas . . . ," she began.

And soon the three homeless orphans were swept up in the fantasy of a Christmas that could exist only in their dreams. It was a family Christmas in a house called a home, with a room ablaze in candlelight. And on a table laid with a clean white cloth, a mother's Christmas pudding sat waiting just for them.

CHAPTER TWENTY-ONE

VERY DAY AT WORK, LUCY MADE THE MOST exquisite hearts. The dolls sold briskly, and Miss Thimblebee smiled appreciatively at her new Hearts Girl. And when Emma teased Lucy that she was becoming Miss Thimblebee's pet, Lucy blushed with delight. She looked forward to her days spent in the company of the kind old woman and her many smiling dolls.

Best of all, though, was closing time. For it was only then, after all the doll makers had gone home, that she and Miss Thimblebee could be alone together. Lucy would happily sit at the counter as Miss Thimblebee tallied up her receipts. The two would talk excitedly about the dolls they had made that day. Miss Thimblebee knew them all by name.

One night, after Miss Thimblebee had gone home, Lucy opened the front door to let Nick and Glory in. Later, as she watched Glory rocking before the fire with Morning Glory in her arms, Lucy's thoughts turned to Miss Thimblebee and the sister she had lost so long ago. *What was the old woman's life like away from the doll shop?* Lucy wondered. With no husband nor children to call her own, how lonely must she be?

It was then that Lucy began to imagine that she and Glory were Miss Thimblebee's own daughters and that they were a family. And though the old woman never did more than bid her good-night, Lucy imagined that, like her own mother in the stories she told, Miss Thimblebee would hug them to her, kissing their foreheads twice, once for love and once for luck. She imagined that Morning Glory was Glory's own doll to keep and that she would never have to give her up.

But as the days passed and Christmas Eve grew closer, Lucy felt a shadow cross her heart, for she knew their time at Thimblebee's was soon coming to an end. Soon the other Hearts Girl, Mary, would be well enough to resume her position. And once again, the Wolcott sisters' uncertain future would be put back into Lucy's hands, a future with no guarantee of a warm stove, a hot supper, or a roof over their heads.

Lucy tried hard not to think about the days to come, wanting only to savor the sweetness of their time at Thimblebee's. But it was on the twenty-third of December, just one day shy of Christmas Eve, that she had to face the bitter fact that her dreams were about to crumble. For while she was in the workroom looking through a basket of floss, Lucy heard Miss Thimblebee call, "Bess, how is our supply of heads?"

Bess searched all the shelves. "We're almost out, mum," she called back.

"Oh, dear," Miss Thimblebee said. "I was afraid of that. Mr. Hippel, our supplier, has just been in to say he shan't have any more for us until after Christmas. Search the shelves again and use whatever you can."

Bess dutifully began tearing through boxes and rummaging through baskets. Lucy froze as she heard her say, "I suppose we'll have to use this old one, even though the mouth is a bit crooked."

Lucy's heart sank. This couldn't be happening!

"Emma, take measurements for a body," Bess ordered. "And I'll see about the hair. Fair, I should think. Iris, we'll leave the dress to you. Blue organdy would do nicely."

But her voice faded into the background as Lucy's heart began to pound wildly in her chest. For as Lucy watched, Thimblebee's head doll-maker opened the scissors that hung from the chain round her neck. And with one swift swipe, she cut off Morning Glory's head!

"Are you quite all right?" Emma asked, on seeing Lucy's face go white.

"Yes," Lucy whispered.

But in truth, she was close to despair, for she knew how Glory's heart was going to break if Morning Glory were to be sold.

As she sat back at her table in the window Lucy looked into the display room to see the many customers making their purchases. She watched as a young girl dressed in a smart green wool coat and velvet bonnet pointed to a doll on a shelf.

"Oh, Papa, I must have her!" the girl cried. "I really must!"

"But, my pet, you have so many dolls already," her father protested. "You couldn't possibly want another."

"Oh, but I do. I do," the girl insisted.

"We shall see. We shall see," replied her father with a smile. "Remember, Christmas is not here yet." Lucy watched as he went up to the counter and whispered in Miss Thimblebee's ear.

And no sooner had the two walked out the door than Miss Thimblebee pulled the doll off the shelf and told Emma to "set her aside."

How is it, Lucy thought grimly, *that some should have so much while others have so little? 'Twas foolish of me to ever think such things as gifts and Christmas cheer were ever meant for orphans like Glory and me.*

Meanwhile, the doll-makers quickened their pace, for the Christmas rush had them working in a frenzy.

It was late in the day when Iris carried the last basket of newly made dolls out to the little table in the display window.

As Lucy reached for the first doll on the pile, her heart skipped a beat, for it was Morning Glory! But the old doll was so transformed, Lucy didn't recognize her at first. The mud-stained moppet was gone! In her place, a fair-faced beauty with long golden curls smiled the familiar smile. Lucy could hardly believe her eyes, for she looked just like the Morning Glory she had imagined in her stories!

This new Morning Glory was dressed in a flounced gown of robin's egg blue to match the color of her eyes. Her petticoats were edged in lace, as was the pinafore that was tied in bows down her back. Around her neck hung a delicate seed-pearl necklace and in her hand she held a straw bonnet with red silk poppies sewn to its brim.

Oh, Morning Glory, Lucy thought. *You are too beautiful!*

"She's quite a sight now, hey?" Iris said. "Too bad about that smile tilting up, though. Bess said if it weren't for that we should ask four shillings. But we've had to price her at three."

Too stunned to speak, Lucy stared down at the doll.

"You best not dawdle," Iris called back over her

shoulder as she returned to the workroom. "We've another four dolls to finish before closing."

With her eyes full of tears, Lucy removed Morning Glory's pinafore and dress. As her finger outlined a heart on the clean white chest, she pondered what color thread to choose. Should it be rose pink, or deep cherry red?

"No, no," Lucy said through her tears, for neither seemed right. And as she gazed down at Morning Glory's smiling face, she thought of her own sweet Glory and the love the child had for the doll. Then suddenly, secretly, she let that love guide her hand.

Lucy hurriedly pulled a strand of blue thread from the basket. Stealing a glance out the window, she was relieved to find no one there. With great speed, she stitched a little morning glory blossom onto the white chest, directly where the heart should go. When she finished, she threaded her needle with a bit of green floss and added two leaves and a stem that twirled in a delicate vine. Then quickly, lest anyone notice, she dressed Morning Glory and set her in a basket with the other finished dolls.

Little did Lucy Wolcott know that with those few stitches of blue and green, with the making of that one delicate blossom, the course of her destiny was to change forever.

At the end of the day, Miss Thimblebee called everyone into the back room.

"It looks to be another good season," she proclaimed. "I'm pleased to announce that we're caught up with our orders. May the miracle of Christmas be with you and your loved ones."

Lucy thought then about her loved one and wondered how the miracle of Christmas could ever find her.

"Of course, you'll all be receiving your Christmas boxes tomorrow," she heard Miss Thimblebee say. "And it being Christmas Eve, we shall keep to our tradition of giving a special gift to our Hearts Girl."

Lucy blinked in surprise.

"She will be allowed to choose the doll of her choice from those that are still on our shelves come closing time, tomorrow." She smiled at Lucy. "So you can begin to consider your choice, and if the doll is still here at closing, she shall be yours."

"Any doll?" Lucy gasped.

"Yes, yes." Miss Thimblebee clucked. "Any one you fancy." Then she rushed through the curtains at the sound of the front doorbells.

"To keep for my very own?" Lucy whispered aloud.

"Yes, your very own," Bess chuckled.

"Any I choose?" Lucy's voice quivered.

"Any that's left," Emma reminded her.

"Don't you worry none, Lucy," Bess was quick to add. "There's always at least three or four left to choose from."

"The sorriest looking ones," Iris noted. "Like that one with the odd smile. I'll wager you'll find her still sitting on the shelf come closing time."

Lucy said a silent prayer that she would be right.

CHAPTER TWENTY-TWO

 HAT NIGHT WHEN GLORY STEPPED INTO THE doll shop, her teeth were chattering so hard she could barely talk. Her cough had grown worse, as the weather had turned bitter. Lucy winced to hear Nick admit they had had another rough day.

Lucy washed the grime from Glory's hands and face and set her before the fire. Later as she set out a potato, Lucy was alarmed to find that Glory had no appetite. Refusing to eat was a sure sign of sickness, but even as ill as she was, Glory still asked for her doll.

With a candle in her hand Lucy guided Glory into the display room to a shelf where six new dolls sat smiling in a row. They were all smartly dressed in fine frocks, with straw bonnets and dainty shoes. Their smiles were of the sweetest variety, all but one, whose lips turned up in a slight curve on one side. Seeing the familiar little smile, Glory let out a gasp.

"Oh, Morning Glory, you are so beautiful!" she

cried. "You look just like Morning Glory in the story!"

Even Nick stepped closer to get a better look. "Are they going to sell her, then?" he asked.

Lucy nodded.

"No, Luce!" Glory cried. "You mustn't let that happen! You mustn't let anyone buy her."

"They may," Lucy said. "But if no one does, she'll be ours!"

"Ours!" Glory gasped.

Lucy grinned and hugged her sister tight. "The Hearts Girl gets any doll of her choice on Christmas Eve," Lucy told her.

"You? You get to choose?" Glory cried.

"I am the Hearts Girl."

"And will you choose Morning Glory?" Glory asked anxiously.

"Well, of course I will!" Lucy exclaimed. "If she's still on the shelf, that is." Lucy went on to explain that she would not be able to make her choice until closing on Christmas Eve.

"Oh, but she looks so lovely now." Glory sighed. "Someone will surely want to buy her."

"Don't you worry none, Glory," Nick said. "She's a sight nicer to look at, 'tis true, but see 'ere, she ain't as perfect as the others. She'll be passed over. You'll see."

"She looks just right to me," Glory said.

"And wait until you see her heart," Lucy whispered, pulling the doll from the shelf. She untied Morning Glory's bows and stays on her pinafore and dress. As Glory held the candle, Lucy pulled back the material to reveal the blue blossom that was stitched where the heart should be.

Glory's face lit up at the sight of it. "Oh, Luce!" she whispered. "'Tis just like the blossoms Mother always made for me!"

"Yes," Lucy said. "It's just the same."

As they made their way through the display room, Glory stopped to look up at the glass case that hung on the wall.

"Sweet dreams, Charlotte," she whispered. "Sweet dreams."

Lucy felt a chill as she heard her little sister's words, for they had been the exact words Miss Thimblebee had whispered. And once again Lucy was seized by the incredible sadness Miss Thimblebee must have endured to lose her dear sister.

That night, Glory slept fitfully, often awakened by her own coughing. Lucy's own dreams were a jumble of hope and heartbreak.

With a light dusting of snow, Christmas Eve morning arrived. Much to Lucy's horror, she discovered that Glory's condition had worsened in the night. The little one's face was flushed with fever and she was so listless Lucy could not get her to stand.

"What shall we do?" Lucy whispered anxiously to Nick.

"I don't know," Nick said, shaking his head. "But if she were to go out in the cold today, I fear she'd not live to see nightfall."

Lucy knew he was right. She knew how fast a sickness could take a child to death's door. What Glory needed now was rest and warmth, two things she would certainly not find out on the cold streets.

"Wot if we was to hide her in 'ere?" Nick suggested.

Frantically, Lucy looked around the back room. But she knew how quiet the doll-makers were as they sewed. All conversation stopped when they were busy. If she were to hide Glory in the back room, surely they'd hear her coughing.

"We must decide now," Nick warned as he peered out the back window. "The charwomen are already making their rounds and Miss Thimblebee will be coming soon."

Lucy hurried out to the display room. "Over here!" she cried, bending down before a little closet door next to the stove. "It's warm here. We'll put her in here."

So with Nick's help Lucy made a little bed for

Glory in the closet, propping her head on a bolt of cotton.

"You must promise me you'll be as quiet as you can, Glory," Lucy said, as she covered her sister with several yards of flannel and the warm quilt.

The little one was so listless she barely managed to nod her drooping head. Lucy walked Nick to the front door to let him out.

"Bring her some tea whenever you can," he whispered. "And, Lucy, when I'm out today, on the church steps, I'll say a prayer there for her. I'd go inside if I could, but the Minister, he don't like us street boys inside his church. But I will be on the steps, and the Lord should hear me from there, being so close to his house, don't you think?"

Lucy was about to answer when the loud crack of a coachman's whip and the sound of horses' hooves caused them both to jump. Without another word, Nick ran for the door and Lucy followed. Once he was gone, she quickly turned the lock.

Back in the display room Lucy opened the little door in the closet and found Glory fast asleep. Reaching out to wrap a finger round one of her golden locks, she stared down at Glory's closed eyes. The skin was so thin and blue, it pained Lucy to look at them, for they looked so like Aggie Crofter's eyelids, eyelids that Lucy knew would never open again.

And suddenly she recalled the washerwoman's words, "With the likes of the sickness going round, I've seen little ones wot were running about on a Monday and come Tuesday they be lying under the grave-digger's shovel."

Lucy leaned over to kiss Glory's forehead, when just then, she heard the expected sound of a key turning in the front-door lock. She quickly shut the closet door and hurried up into the display window.

"Merry Christmas to you, my dear," Miss Thimblebee called out cheerily as she stepped into the display room.

Chapter Twenty-Three

S SNOWFLAKES DRIFTED OVER LONDON'S cobbled streets, and the ringing church bells filled the frosty air, the spirit of Christmas made itself known throughout the city. But nowhere was the magic of the season more apparent that Christmas Eve morning than in the quirky little building that stood at Number Nine Mulberry Lane.

For inside the tiny doll shop a buzz of excitement could be felt by all, as one by one the smiling dolls were lifted from the lace-lined shelves and gingerly laid in tissue, boxed, and wrapped with ribbon. Miss Thimblebee was so busy with the steady stream of shoppers who had come in search of a Thimblebee's doll that Lucy and Iris were enlisted to help behind the counter.

As Iris showed Lucy how to wrap a package, it was all Lucy could do to contain her fear. What if someone should hear Glory cough or call out? What if one of the doll-makers should need a bolt of material from the storage space? What if Glory's sickness should grow worse and she were to die, alone in the dark closet?

Lucy had hoped to bring cups of tea to Glory as often as she could, but when she was almost caught after the second cup, she didn't dare try it again.

Added to all of Lucy's worries was the threat that Morning Glory could be sold. For as the shop filled with last-minute customers, Lucy knew that Glory's doll could be carried off at any minute. But she calmed herself by remembering Iris's words, "I'll wager she'll be sitting on the shelf come Christmas Eve."

The constant jangle of bells filled the air as Thimblebee's plum door swung open and closed.

"I think we'll be needing more ribbon," Miss Thimblebee said as she tied a big green bow around a package.

"There's none left in the back room," Iris told her.

"Well, then, fetch some from the storage closet," Miss Thimblebee ordered. "I'm sure I put some in there last week."

"I'll go, mum," Lucy cried, racing around the counter.

"Who put a bee in her bonnet?" Iris remarked.

"Must be the excitement of the Christmas season." Miss Thimblebee smiled.

Lucy hurried over to the storage closet and carefully opened it just enough so that no one could see in. With the display room bustling with customers, the others were much too busy to notice her. She quickly reached in and felt for Glory's hand.

"Are you all right?" she whispered into the darkened closet. There was no reply save for the little hand that squeezed her own.

"You've been so very good," Lucy whispered. "It won't be long now. You go on and rest. I'll be back soon." She pulled a card of ribbon out and brought it back to the counter.

As she stood and wrapped a box, Lucy held her breath at the sight of Morning Glory still sitting on the shelf. Nervously, she watched as each customer paused to have a look at the doll.

When one woman with a basketful of parcels went so far as to lift her from the shelf, it was all Lucy could do to keep from shouting, "No!"

But when a silk-gowned doll caught the woman's eye, she roughly set Morning Glory back down. Lucy breathed a short sigh of relief, before the panic set back in. There were so few dolls left, she was certain each new customer would sweep Morning Glory away. And so the minutes dragged by until it was almost closing. The doll-makers had been let go early so they could enjoy the holiday with their families. Lucy and Miss Thimblebee were alone behind the counter when a young minister stepped through the door.

Oh, do let him be the last customer, thought Lucy, as she and Miss Thimblebee watched him reach for the last two baby dolls on the shelf.

"They're going to a good home. He's the proud father of twin girls," Miss Thimblebee commented. "I daresay, with the snow coming down as it is, we shan't see any more customers today." She smiled as she looked over the many empty shelves. "Why, there are only three dolls left! I'm afraid they are not the best of the lot. But is there one that takes your fancy, dear?"

Lucy's heart was near bursting as she looked for the hundredth time that day to Morning Glory, who was sitting in her usual spot.

"Yes!" Lucy cried. "Oh, yes, there is."

"Very good." Miss Thimblebee nodded as she pulled down the shade and locked the door.

"So, which shall it be, my child?"

Lucy lifted her hand to point to Morning Glory when a loud rattling of wheels sounded from out on the street. Miss Thimblebee and Lucy turned to look out of the display window.

"My stars!" Miss Thimblebee exclaimed.

For there outside stood a magnificent coach with two white horses and footmen dressed in livery. An elegantly dressed lady stepped down from the coach and came to the door.

Lucy's heart stopped as Miss Thimblebee whispered, "She's coming to our shop! It seems we have one last customer."

Miss Thimblebee unlocked the door and hurried back to the counter. A few moments later, the woman stepped into the display room. From the rich scent of her perfume and the swish of her sumptuous satin dress, Lucy knew that she must be a high-born lady indeed.

"Oh, dear," the woman said. "Her Majesty will be quite disappointed." She sighed as she scanned the empty shelves.

"Her Majesty?" Miss Thimblebee gasped.

"Yes," the woman replied. "For I have been sent by the Queen. You see, the daughter of Her Majesty's gardener is gravely ill and Her Majesty wishes to send the poor child a gift. We've heard of your marvelous dolls with their special hearts and I promised to bring one back."

"I'm most honored you chose our shop," Miss Thimblebee said proudly.

"We've come quite a distance from the palace," the woman said, taking a quick glance about the shop. "But you seem to be all sold out."

"Oh, my, I'm afraid you've come quite late," Miss

Thimblebee cried, clasping her hands to her cheeks. "But maybe you would like one of these that are left."

Taking a step forward in her fine kid-leather shoes, the lady suddenly stopped and stared at the three remaining dolls. Lucy held her breath as she watched the lady's satin-cuffed sleeve glide along the shelf from one doll to the next.

"No, these won't do at all," the lady said dryly.

Lucy breathed a sigh of relief, until she saw that the glass case that hung on the wall had caught the woman's eye.

"What have we here?" she asked.

Miss Thimblebee turned pale, as the lady stepped behind the counter and asked that the case be opened.

"I would gladly show you that doll, Your Ladyship, but . . . but . . . ," Miss Thimblebee stammered as she put the key into the tiny brass lock. "But as you can plainly read, the sign says NOT FOR SALE."

"Not for sale to the Queen?"

"Well, of course, for the Queen," Miss Thimblebee began. "But, you see, this doll . . . this doll . . ."

"Yes, what about this doll?" the woman asked impatiently.

"'Tis nothing." Miss Thimblebee's voice was barely a whisper as she reached for Charlotte and lifted her from the case.

Lucy's own heart was breaking at the sight of the old woman's trembling fingers as she laid Charlotte down on a sheet of clean brown paper.

Not Charlotte! Lucy thought. Poor Miss Thimblebee could never bear to lose her. How could such a thing happen?

As Lucy stood helplessly by, a sudden *creak* sounded in the display room. Everyone turned to see the little closet door beside the stove open a crack.

"Mercy me!" Miss Thimblebee cried on seeing a little head of tangled blonde curls peek out.

"Glory!" Lucy gasped, and rushed to the closet door. Then she wrapped her arms around the feverish child. " 'Tis my little sister, mum."

Without a word, Glory pulled away from her sister's arms and made her way across the room. Standing on tiptoe, she lifted Morning Glory from off the shelf.

The little one's big blue eyes filled with tears as she carried the doll back to Lucy. She looked down at Morning Glory and then to Miss Thimblebee, whose own wrinkled hand rested on Charlotte.

"Go ahead," Glory whispered as she held Morning Glory out to Lucy.

"But Glory," Lucy whispered back. "She's your doll."

"Yes, and she always will be," Glory replied, fighting back her tears. "But there's another whose heart aches far more than mine." She looked over sadly at Miss Thimblebee.

And at that moment, Lucy understood exactly what her sister meant for her to do.

"Begging your pardon, my lady," Lucy said. "But there is one doll that you haven't seen. This doll," she said, lifting Morning Glory from Glory's arms.

"Why, of course, I saw that one," the lady sighed. "She's quite ordinary."

"Yes, at first glance she does seem like an ordinary doll," Lucy agreed. "But if you'll look closer," she said, untying Morning Glory's pinafore, "you'll find that she is quite rare. For here is a heart you'll not find on another."

With that, Lucy revealed the little blossom that was so perfectly sewn on the doll's cloth chest.

"Exquisite!" the lady murmured.

"Why, Lucy!" Miss Thimblebee exclaimed with alarm. "That is not a standard Thimblebee heart!"

Lucy lowered her eyes, suddenly ashamed.

Meanwhile, the lady extended a ringed finger and touched a curl of Morning Glory's hair. "Not standard?" she said. "A heart like no other? Rare, you say?"

Glory poked her head out from behind Lucy's skirts, and the two sisters nodded.

"In that case, I shall have this one, rather than the other," the lady announced. "For the Queen prizes rare above all else. If this doll's heart be that rare, 'twill please Her Highness greatly. How much does she cost?"

"Why, why, there's no charge, my lady," Miss Thimblebee cried, hardly able to conceal her relief. "You do me a great honor to deliver one of our dolls to Her Majesty, and I require no payment for that."

Miss Thimblebee quickly wrapped Morning Glory and handed her to the lady-in-waiting. With a smile, the woman put the package into her large velvet bag, and snapped the purse's silver clasp shut.

The sound rang in Lucy's ears, as deadly as if she had snapped Morning Glory's neck, as deadly as if she'd snapped Glory's little heart in two.

Chapter Twenty-Four

NCE THE LADY HAD LEFT THE SHOP, MISS Thimblebee locked the door and returned to the counter where the two girls stood trembling. Miss Thimblebee gazed in silence from one sister to the other. What was she going to do? Certainly they would be sent back to Grimstone now.

"So, Lucy Wolcott, you have a little sister," the old woman broke the silence. "Why ever didn't you tell me about this child?"

Lucy felt her own cheeks grow hot with shame. "I know 'twas wrong of me," she admitted. "But you said I wasn't to let anyone into the shop at night. We're orphans, you see, with no family of any kind, and 'tis up to me to look after her. She was so sick, and your stove was so very warm."

"Orphans? Sick?" Miss Thimblebee exclaimed, noticing Glory's flushed cheeks for the first time. "Oh, my, you're quite feverish. You must be put to bed at once!"

"And I'm sorry about the blossom for the doll's heart," Lucy continued, speaking quickly. " 'Twas another wrong, I know. But I only . . . , "

"She only did it for me," Glory spoke up in a little voice.

" 'Twas on account of the story I told her," Lucy tried to explain. "A story about a doll our mother had given her. A doll called Morning Glory."

"But the doll was lost when Mother died," Glory went on. "Lucy always said I would find her one day and I did. She was waiting for me down by the river."

"Waiting for you down by the river?" Miss Thimblebee repeated.

"I didn't think it would do any harm," Lucy whispered. "She's had so little in her life. And when we found the doll, why, Glory came to think of her as her own. So when it was time to make the doll's heart, I sewed a morning glory there, just the way our mother would have done. I don't imagine you can ever forgive me. So if you please, mum, we'll be on our way."

But Miss Thimblebee didn't dismiss them. Instead she stood silently, lost in her thoughts. "You must be quite sad, my child," she said, looking down at Glory, "to see a doll you so loved be taken away."

Glory nodded, as the sadness at losing her doll washed over her.

"But as sad as she is," Lucy said, "she'd be sadder still if she thought you were to lose your Charlotte."

Miss Thimblebee's eyebrows arched high over her spectacles. "Charlotte? What do you know of my Charlotte?"

Lucy told Miss Thimblebee how they had come to know the story of her sister's beautiful doll. "For you see mum, 'tis a mighty heart that beats in my little sister's chest."

As Lucy spoke, Miss Thimblebee blinked back her own tears. For she was beginning now to understand the depth of the gift the girls had just given to her.

With a wave of her hand, she beckoned to them to come close. Glory let go of Lucy's skirts, and they cautiously approached Miss Thimblebee. She placed one arm around Lucy and the other around Glory, and she opened her heart and let the children in.

"Mighty," Miss Thimblebee repeated softly, kissing them each on the forehead. "Yes, mighty indeed." And she hugged them both close to her bosom, as only a mother could do.

Chapter Twenty-Five

 N HEARING A *RAP-RAP-RAP* AT THE DISPLAY window, Lucy looked up to see Nick, his paper cap covered in snow.

"'Tis our friend, Nick Button, looking for us," Lucy told Miss Thimblebee. "I suppose we should be going now." Lucy opened the door.

"This child can't be going back out in that cold," Miss Thimblebee insisted, gently smoothing back Glory's curls. "She needs some hot soup and a warm place by the fire — and a doctor if she's to get well. And this one hasn't got proper shoes or stockings," she said, looking over at Nick. "Besides, have you really got a place to go?"

"No," Lucy admitted.

"Good, 'tis settled," Miss Thimblebee said.

"Then . . . then we can stay the night in the shop?"

"Stay the night? In the shop? On Christmas Eve? I should say not!"

■　　■　　■

Much later that evening, as the snow silently drifted from one London rooftop to another, six blackbirds spread their wings over Mulberry Lane. 'Twas a short flight they made that frosty Christmas Eve night in the hush of a winter's snow. Their destination, a peak beside the smoking chimney pots atop Number Fourteen, for they sensed it a good, warm place to rest their wings.

Meanwhile, below the snowy rooftop was a happy little group who gathered around a table brimming with good cheer. With a roaring fire in the grate and the room ablaze in candlelight, a radiant Miss Thimblebee sat down to share her holiday feast with three grateful guests.

After dinner, Miss Thimblebee took the stocking that was hanging from her mantel and made a present of it to the one who was in need of it most.

"'Tis the very best season of all," Nick crowed, as he happily emptied the stocking on the table, sharing the contents of nuts and oranges with all who were there. Then he kicked off his shoe and with a look of utmost pleasure he slipped his bare foot into the warm wool sock.

Miss Thimblebee next placed a box before Lucy. It was wrapped in brown paper and tied with a plum-colored bow.

"This one is for you to give your sister," she whispered. "Go on, give it to her."

Lucy did as she was told. With an anxious tug, Glory pulled the ribbon loose and opened the box. Both girls gasped at the sight of the beautiful Charlotte within.

"I know 'tis not the doll you would have wished for, my dear child," Miss Thimblebee apologized. "But it would mean so much to me if you would take her as your own. She hasn't been in a little one's arms in a very long time."

Lucy held her breath as she watched Glory's large blue eyes peering over the box.

Oh, if only it could have been her Morning Glory instead, Lucy thought.

But much to her surprise, a smile crept over Glory's face as she reached for Charlotte and lifted her into her arms.

"Merry Christmas, Charlotte," Glory said, holding the doll close. Then she lowered her voice to a whisper. "And Merry Christmas, Morning Glory, wherever you are."

Lucy understood then what the wisest have always known, that the true miracle of Christmas is not in the getting, but the giving. And in her heart she felt a warm, happy glow.

"Oh, my stars!" Miss Thimblebee cried, bursting from her seat and bustling into the kitchen. "Why, I'd almost forgotten dessert!"

The air soon filled with the spicy scent of cinnamon and nutmeg and the sweet aroma of a pudding. For as Lucy turned to look, she saw Miss Thimblebee coming from the kitchen, carrying a silver tray.

"Make room, make room," the kind old woman clucked as she set a steaming plum pudding down on the table's clean white cloth.

As the evening came to a close, Miss Thimblebee lifted her cup of punch in a toast. "Merry Christmas, my dears," she said with a smile.

"Yes, it is," Lucy declared, as she lifted her cup. "'Tis the merriest Christmas of all!"

Epilogue

 ET US RETURN ONCE MORE TO THAT FROSTY rooftop and the black-winged creatures that took refuge there. 'Tis said that black-birds are the wisest of their kind, and in truth, it must be so. For Number Fourteen Mulberry Lane proved a most warm and welcoming place to both the weary wings atop and the tired feet below.

And so it was that the flight of two orphaned sis-ters came to the sweetest of ends, as Miss Thimble-bee opened her heart and her house to shelter the two from the harsh winter winds. Lucy and Glory were adopted as Miss Thimblebee's own. With proper food and loving care, the girls grew healthy and strong. They went on to work happily together in the doll shop for many years to come.

It was also Nick Button's good fortune not to be left out in the cold. For he found himself a home as well, just down the lane at Number Fifteen. It was there that Thimblebee's head doll-maker, the kind-hearted Bess, and her husband offered to take him in.

From then on, the only tumbling Nick did was to amuse Lucy and Glory, who remained his very dear friends.

As for Charlotte, she was never to spend another lonely night in her glass case, but slept each night in Glory's loving arms instead. And though the little one thought often of her Morning Glory, she took comfort in knowing the gift she gave so freely gladdened more hearts than one.

Which leaves us with one last heart to account for, one most rare and carefully stitched. What happened to that delicate little blossom? Where had Morning Glory finally come to rest? She found her way to where she was most needed, the very place flowers grow best. She found her way to a beautiful garden and a young girl whose own heart had grown weary and worn.

For in a thatched cottage, beside the Queen's own sleeping roses, a dying child lay. She was her father's favorite, Lily, no longer strong enough to walk the garden path. It was on Christmas morning that the package from the palace arrived. And when Morning Glory was gently placed beside the sick child's bed, the crooked little smile did not fail to work its magic. But it was the rare blossom of a heart that seemed to have the greatest effect.

Many have said 'twas the love Lily felt for her new

Christmas doll that suddenly caused her condition to turn. For she was, after all, a gardener's daughter, and it was not surprising then that such a special flower should put her on the mend.

And though she never discovered the seamstress of the blossom nor the one who had the mighty heart to give it away, she would have been most happy to know it was a gardener's own two daughters who wished her and the sweet Morning Glory a merry Christmas Day.